THE BIRD HAS NO WINGS

THE BIRD HAS NO WINGS

Letters of Peter Schwiefert

Edited by
Claude Lanzmann

Translated by Barbara Lucas

Search Press London

First published in Great Britain
in 1976
by Search Press Limited
2–10 Jerdan Place London SW6 5PT

Published originally in
French by Éditions Gallimard, Paris

Printed and bound in the United States of America
ISBN 0 85532 361 2

Peter Schwiefert was killed in 1945 at the age of twenty-seven. These private letters are the sum total of his legacy. It was his ambition to be a writer, but the period in which he lived his short life hardly gave him the time, what with his sheer struggle for survival as a penniless emigrant and then his active service in the war. The following sixty letters written to his mother—all, except the last, between December, 1938, and March, 1941—make a poignant document, rendered still more striking by their completely personal nature; they reveal a young man who was totally immersed in the events around him and who bore witness to them, as it were in spite of himself.

These letters are evidence not only of the tragedies and disruptions of emigration and of the way various members of a German family reacted to Nazism; they also show us a Jewish mother being ardently questioned by her half-Jewish son—a mother passionately loved yet ceaselessly challenged, interrogated, called on to make a choice, called on to show herself equal to a situation she was unable or unwilling to bring herself to face. The son turned his back on compromise and took on himself the responsibility of being a Jew, whereas the mother seemed to vacillate; the son was led to a radical refusal, and lived out its consequences.

That was enough, in the circumstances of the time, to generate an exemplary and tragic destiny.

Peter Schwiefert's first letter, dated 6 December 1938, was written from a small Portuguese village called Faro. He had left his native Berlin at the end of the previous October. He had supposed that Portugal would be no more than a stepping stone as his ultimate intention was to emigrate to South America. But as he was only twenty-one and had no money or skills, he was forced to stay on in Portugal. He spent his first months there in near-destitution. His father (the playwright Fritz Schwiefert) and his stepfather (his mother's third husband, referred to in these letters as "Uncle Schr"[1]*) looked on his decision as unnecessary, not to say irresponsible. They could not understand why someone with a thoroughly German surname, and whom they had guaranteed to protect, should choose exile of his own free will, and they refused him all financial help. Even his mother questioned the sincerity of his motives. From his very first letter Peter's anxiety is manifest; less than a month before, during the night of 9–10 November — the famous "Crystal Night" — the hunting-down of Jews had reached a climax in Germany; an all-out pogrom on a nationwide basis had been organized by the government itself. With no news from his mother, Peter Schwiefert feared the worst. But he also feared that she might not be prepared to risk her chance of remaining in Berlin by taking an adverse stand. It is true that his mother hoped right up till the last moment that she would be*

[1]Peter's mother—an extremely attractive and popular woman in Berlin—had three children, Peter, Bettina, and Angelika, from three different Germans, all non-Jews. But when this correspondence began she was already separated from her third husband, Erich Schrobsdorff, with whom she nevertheless still maintained a close relationship.

able to slip through the net on account of her Christian marriages. Her third husband did all he could to protect her and her two daughters. "Crystal Night" marked the end of these illusions, as the Nazis intended it to do. The most assimilated, the most respectable, even the blindest of German Jews now had to bow to the fact that they would not escape from the common fate. A few weeks after her son's voluntary departure, the mother had to envisage her own necessary emigration. Where, when, and how she would go she did not yet know. But one can see that she already had death in her soul.

Angelika Schrobsdorff, Peter's half-sister and herself a writer, allowed me to read these letters in Jerusalem and gave me permission to translate and publish them.

Faro, 6 December 1938

Dearest Mother,

I'm terribly worried. Has anything happened? I've been without news for nearly a month now. Please don't leave me in this anxiety. I'm not so far away, you know, as to be unaware of what's going on. Have they started harassing you yet? Are you ill? Please, please write at once, if only a few lines.

I hope to get a letter by return post and am always close to you in my thoughts. Be brave, my dearest, and have faith that things will change. They will. They always do. Oh, if only my love could help you in any way at all! But how silly I am—it can only contribute to my own suffering.

Listen, I want to tell you something from the bottom of my heart: don't disown or condemn your and your own children's Jewishness. It's your whole strength. That doesn't mean that you have to prepare yourself for martyrdom. All you have to do is to love what has been given you as an honour. Because that's what it is. A grave responsibility. Don't forget that you can escape from everything, but never from yourself.

With my most fervent prayers for all of you,
Your Peter

Faro, 10 December 1938

Dearest Mother,

I understand and shall say no more.

I didn't know about it in such detail. I only had vague news, rumours that reached me without my really taking them in, without giving them the importance they deserved. But your letter has now enlightened me. I'm ashamed now of having thought only of myself and of having therefore forgotten all the rest. Is it too late?

I've got work already. I'm giving German lessons. And I'm hoping to extend this activity by getting pupils in town. I'll do what I can and if the lessons don't work then I'll find something else. I've cut down expenses to the barest minimum. I want to help you, I'm entirely at your disposal. If you need me, if you think I can be useful to you in any way, you only have to write and I shall come at once, I promise. Everything I have belongs to you, and I would like you also to bear in mind Lisbon and my house. It's a possibility.

I've written you two long letters which you obviously haven't received. I've been waiting for yours for weeks. I've not had a word from Liena[2] either. Perhaps my letters simply aren't arriving. I say again in all sincerity: neither I nor my personal wishes have the slightest importance now. All sympathy for me is superfluous.

What you really must recognise is that my "romantic dreams" of departure and independence (as you call them) would have had a justification even in other circumstances. After all I was alone, I depended on no one's support, I had to discover my own path, work out

[2]Liena, the girl he loved.

my own rule of life.[3] Everything is changed now because I'm not alone any more. I've understood everything and only want to help, to support, to play my part, as far as is in my power.

Write to me, kiss the children and kiss your parents. I'm always close to you.

With infinite hope and love.
Your Peter

Faro, 20 December 1938

Darling Mother,

There's not much to say. I can't put my hopes into words. All I hope is that you may have a little peace. And I implore you all to love me as I love you. I'd like to prove my love, not just confine myself to words. I want to do everything, absolutely everything, to be a good son and brother. I'm very close to you now and realise that we can't be separated. You weigh too heavy. Oh, there's nothing I can say. So what can I tell you? Be strong and hold your head high. There's only one thing I think about and that is helping you, helping you all with my whole strength! Perhaps some time you will need me. It would be the best present you could give me.

All my wishes for the new year, and all my hopes for what lies in store for you.

[3] Peter Schwiefert was first brought up by his parents, then by his maternal grandparents. Later he went to a boarding school, then returned to his mother's home for a short time (she had remarried and his relations with his stepfather were stormy). Then he lived alone until he left Berlin.

I've just received a letter from Uncle Schr. I won't go into the details, the outrageous insinuations, falsifications, and offensive remarks in his "witty" version of thoughts I've never had and declarations I've never made. I don't intend to hit back. I'm utterly indifferent to what these gentlemen in Germany think about me. And I'm just as indifferent to them personally. It's a long time since I owed any of them anything, and as for the concern they've "always" shown for me, I utterly repudiate it. Let them go to the devil with their "advice" and leave me in peace. I want nothing from them, nothing, nor from anyone else. As for their suggestion that I hoped to obtain through my letters some kind of "financial share", it's sheer impudence. I don't need anything, as fortunately I've laid my plans better than these gentlemen thought possible of an idle versifier. And I shan't write any more letters "with a philosophical substructure" (what a magnificent expression!) which might upset them. I've learned my lesson. My only regret is that I haven't been able to make *you* understand me—not that it's very important now.

Nevertheless to you, and to you alone, I want to emphasise two things. First, that I wasn't properly informed because I don't read a paper and seldom go to town, so I got to know of events only by chance and after considerable delay. And as I've already told you, the news was pretty vague and I quite simply didn't understand what it was all about, God knows why. Perhaps I was asleep. Or else, being so cut off, I was unable to grasp the novelty of the situation and how it differed from the past. Whether it was all these things combined, or something else, I really don't know. What I do know is that it wasn't in any way a desire not to understand or the selfishness of someone who refuses to see things as they are. The other point: I dread not being able to help you. You know my position, and it's now useless to think it could have been otherwise. I tried in my first letter to tell you something about my chances of work. You know I've not learned any skills so you can understand how limited my possibilities are—at best, and this would need a miracle, they would only keep my head above water. Add to this the fact that up till now and probably for several weeks more my hands have been tied because my position has not yet been regularised from the legal point of view, so that I can't get a work permit of any kind. These are the facts.

So the only thing I can offer is my absolute good will. I can only put at your disposal what I actually have. And unfortunately this is no more than my hands and the small amount of intelligence I know myself to have. If these can be of use to you in any way you only have to say so and I shall come. But even if you don't need me—and I really am powerless at the moment—I would try everything on the practical level so as to help you.

One other thing—in future I shall address myself just to you, your children[4] and your parents. I want to think only of you. I want to show my love only to you, whether you understand me or not and whatever you may think of me. As for the others, they can spare me their advice and their warnings just as for my part I shall do everything I can to forget them. They are of absolutely no interest to me and I reject everything that comes from them. I willingly take on myself the odium of ingratitude, for considering the image they have of me, that no longer enters into our accounts.

[4]His two half-sisters, Angelika and Bettina, then aged eleven and fifteen respectively.

As you have shown them my letters up till now, mind you also show them everything I have just said, because it concerns them.

Forgive me, my darlings, for ending like this. I think about you the whole time. I am all yours and kiss you all tenderly.

Your Peter

Faro, 20 January 1939

Dearest Mother,

I've been in Lisbon for a fortnight dealing with the business of my work permit which was dragging on endlessly, like all bureaucratic things. Although the trip wasn't very agreeable, because so expensive, it was necessary and at last I've obtained the necessary authorization.

So I shall give German and English lessons in Olhao and Faro; if I can start on 1 February and get enough pupils, I would take the bus every evening and go into town. I also hope to get translations. But it's all going to take time.

I've had no more news from you! What is your state of mind? Are you bearing up all right? You'll see, everything will be all right and you'll laugh later at all your doubts and worries.

Now I want to tell you about a decision I've made, a decision of great importance to me. I intend to be a convert to Judaism. My intention is firm and unshakable. I've given the matter much thought and have come to the conclusion that this is what I must do—to make my position clear and as it should be. I *am* a Jew, I belong to you and yours, and I want to signify outwardly that this is so.[5] I know very well what it involves; I'm setting out along the same road as all the others, and it's a hard one. But why, by what right, should I be privileged. I want no favour, however small. You know what I think, you know how I've always felt a deep affinity with all things Jewish. I see no difference and do not recognise one. For me conversion is natural and necessary . . . I don't want to delay or let myself be deflected any longer. I'm simply fulfilling a duty towards myself. It is not a religious conversion. I know nothing about the Christian religion or the Jewish religion. But Judaism as such is the only form of Jewish life and there's no other possible way of bearing witness to it. So I shall do all that is possible.

I've had to smile more than once at the strange way Jews have reacted to my decision. They all implore me to go back on it. But always for practical reasons. In any case it's impossible for me to put through the formalities here in Portugal. I talked to a member of the Sephardic community. He harped on my motives and looked at me as if I were some curious kind of animal. Especially as I was a Christian! "We don't accept anyone," he said finally. Then he went off shaking his head. He must be a very good Jew.

So there was only one thing left for me to do (and this involves some practical changes, but of another kind). On 15 January I deposited at the German Consulate in Lisbon a declaration in due form by the terms of which I express my desire to be a convert to Judaism and to carry through this wish just as soon as possible. In the same declaration I asked to be regarded henceforth as a Jew and to be subject to all the laws concerning Jews.

If this declaration is considered valid in Berlin, the

[5]Circumcision. Cf. Ilse Hirsch's letter of 1 August 1945.

letter "J" will be inscribed on my passport and I shall be given "Israel" as a first name.[6] That will make me an emigrant in perpetuity and I shall never be able to return to Germany. And after a while German nationality will be withdrawn from me. That's what they told me at the Consulate.

What the procedure is in these circumstances I don't yet know. In any case the conversion will be official just as soon as a community is prepared to receive me.

My cat, Nicky, has died, if you can believe it. He probably died of food poisoning and it was already too late when I took him to the vet. He died in my arms on the way back from town. Southerners are incredibly cruel where animals are concerned. They weren't at all worried about him but simply said, "Yes, yes, he's going to die, never mind, we'll get you another one." They all laughed when I took him to the vet. I could have killed those women.

Take care of yourself, my dearest, and let me have your news soon. I need it so much! I'm always close to you and I kiss you.

Your Peter

Faro, 21 January 1939

Dear Father,

I want to tell you the following:

On 14 January I deposited at the German Consulate in Lisbon an official declaration by the terms of

[6]One of the "November decrees" promulgated in Nazi Germany after the "Crystal Night" pogrom laid down that all Jews should henceforth have the same first name—for men, Sarah for women.

which I express my desire to be a convert to Judaism and to carry out this wish as soon as possible, and I ask in consequence to be regarded henceforth as a Jew and to have the legislation concerning Jews applied to me.

If this declaration is considered valid in Berlin the letter "J" will be inscribed on my passport and I shall be given the first name of Israel. Then I shall be freed from all my obligations towards the German Reich (for instance regarding military service). I shall become an emigrant in perpetuity and shall never be able to return to Germany. It's also probable that German nationality will be withdrawn from me.

I'm giving you this information to prepare you for any questions that may be put to you unexpectedly and for any annoyance you may be caused as a result.

Your Peter

Faro, 21 January 1939

Dearest Mother,

Many thanks for your letter. Forgive me for sending this to Liena to pass on to you, but stamps are terribly expensive and I have to economise.

How did your Christmas go? Was it a very hard one for you? For me, a real "celebration" was out of the question, but that didn't really matter. I stayed at home, that is to say with Carmo and her two children, my landlady Rosaria and her daughter, and the servant Antonio — who is simplicity itself. As you see, we're already absolutely united and form as it were a single bloc in the Marina community. In fact I occupy, somewhat against my will, a privileged position, almost patriarchal, and am the object of all sorts of attentions. Moreover since 15 December I've been taking my meals at the family table and Carmo looks after me admirably.

I played the part of Father Christmas and distributed small presents to the great delight of the children who would otherwise have received nothing. I pleased the ladies by giving each of them a photograph of myself at their urgent request. The photographs now adorn the various rooms and are the pride of their possessors. My sack being empty, the festivities would have then come to an end if we hadn't suddenly had the idea of going into town to midnight mass. In this way I heard and saw the first mass of my life. To tell the truth it made a poor impression. The church wasn't really ugly, but the saints with their expressionless faces and clad in gleaming red finery, and especially Saint Sebastian in his knight's armour, are quite intolerable. And there was no sense of awe, everything was too fussy, and the choir had manifestly never heard of rhythm. Only one of the servers, who bobbed up and down like a Shakespearian clown, was remarkable. Yes, there's something odd about the organization of churches; I saw clearly on this occasion how absurd they basically are, and how little they have to do with God (even the Catholic God).

Nothing special to say about new year. It passed quietly. There's nothing much to say about me either. Things aren't easy, you know, and everything takes a terribly long time. But I shall pull through. When you say that my difficulties are drawing me nearer to the goal, yes, I've known that for some time. I didn't want to protect myself from them, but I had made my own time schedule. That this has been upset is not really important because lots of things have changed. Besides,

I'm not losing more than I've won, and if one realises that, then everything that happens is necessary, and what is most unforeseen and seemingly hard to take is precisely what we most need.

Lots of kisses to the children and the grandparents. And to you.

Your Peter

It was very late when Peter's mother decided to emigrate. The condition for leaving Germany was that she change her nationality. Her husband, Erich Schrobsdorff ("Uncle Schr"), had business relations with Bulgaria—an Axis country allied to Germany—and he persuaded a Bulgarian bachelor, Dimiter Lingorska, to contract a marriage of convenience with his wife. A marriage of convenience, but endowed—the Bulgarian was paid. The Schrobsdorffs were divorced, and the mother was heartbroken. In order to arouse no suspicions her marriage with Dimiter had to take place in church. Thus she began to study the Russian Orthodox religion and became acquainted with "Father John", a Russian prince who had become a priest. "Father John" exercised such fascination over this Jewish woman on the verge of despair that she soon saw both him and his faith as a way to salvation. A situation that had originally been one of pure opportunism grew into a mystical crisis. She was baptized and married by the priest in the Russian Orthodox Church. For Peter, who was asserting his conversion to Judaism while his mother was embracing the Christian religion, the whole state of affairs was "grotesque".

Faro, 13 February 1939

Dear Mother,

I'm terribly worried about your nervous depression, even though you say you've got the better of it. Please, please tell me the truth. Are you really better? I implore you to tell me exactly how you are. You can imagine how worried I am. Can't you try to concentrate entirely on the future? In that way you could deaden the present and rob it of its most dangerous influence. You must force yourself not to let it weigh on you more than is necessary. It's the only solution remaining to you, for the consequences in themselves are hardly surprising.

And please, please answer my constant questions about your situation. For me questions haven't merely a generalized and natural interest, but a very immediate one. I've got to know what it's all about. People in our position are always finding themselves faced with decisions that have to be made, which is why we have to start with a clear view of things. I'm sure you don't intend to drive a wedge between us. I personally attach the greatest possible importance to keeping permanently in touch with you, and not only for my sake. But these things don't really need saying. So I ask you very solemnly, and you must be good and answer: What are you going to do with Angelika and Bettina?

As for me I have no plans that are not known to you. I'm staying on here of course and only hope that my "teaching activities" will expand. At the moment they're on a very small scale but that's probably because of Carnival. In March things will look up, at least that's what everyone tells me.

And now to this "grotesque" story.

First of all I want you to know that what really matters (to me, too) is that it has helped you to overcome your depression, helped you to get better, which is what you needed so much. Your health comes before everything.

I wanted to start by making this point—and it's the truth—because there are many other things I want to say and I'm not quite sure what they're going to be.

Your irony is unworthy of you and doesn't touch me on the raw as you thought it would. You oughtn't to make fun of other people's decisions when your own, viewed objectively, could be not so much derided as deplored.

Your irony has something uncontrolled about it. You know very well that you're lying to yourself even when you persistently maintain that it's I who am going in for self-deception. Perhaps you no longer have a choice, perhaps it's become inevitable for you—but it's just the opposite in my case. By this I mean that you cannot do otherwise than look for your salvation in cynicism, as always happens with people who haven't a very solid position.

For—to look at things objectively again—there is no real necessity for baptism. The necessity never existed even in the most barbarous epochs, compared with which ours, in spite of everything, is just a nursery game. You know that, and it's why you take refuge in obscurantism. The step you have taken could be justified at a pinch on one condition only—that it "has no importance really" and is primarily indicative of astute opportunism. For what you think to be your strongest argument is in fact your weakest. Your alleged inclination for Catholicism, the benefit you derive from this "liaison"—which brings you peace and comfort as well as aesthetic satisfaction—has lost its justification. It's all false because it's a choice of the moment, a fact I think you haven't realised. For six years you refrained from doing anything whatever about it because it wasn't "necessary". If you had become a Catholic during that long period then the whole thing would be a simple matter of faith and there would be nothing more to say. But although there's been no question of religious belief for five years, and particularly now, you suddenly remember this outgrown desire of yours and build it up into a supplementary justification. It's obvious that now it can't be, and isn't, a matter of belief—with you any more than with me or with anyone else. Because the whole question has evolved in a political direction and has become a general question instead of a personal one. It's no longer a matter of Judaism or Christianity but solely of "Hep-Hep".[7]

And this is not aimed at the Jewish *religion,* as in the days of the Inquisition, but at the Jew as such. The order is: Beat the Jew! and he's beaten. The Jew can let himself be hit, he can hit back, or he can smile and ask, "What are you doing to me?" He can protest, he can pray, he can be clever and get away, he can be prudent and avoid showing himself in the street in the first place, he can react according to the whole spectrum of human reactions. There's just one thing he can't do. He can't say, I'm not what you think I am. Because he is, and will be so for as long as he lives. Whether he's Jewish or Catholic by religion, whether he's a cosmopolitan or an ardent German patriot, whether he's Lord Beaconsfield or Moses Mosessohn of Frankfurter Street, whether he loves, hates, accepts, glories in, or execrates his Jewishness, whether he has twenty Jewish grandparents or . . . is a half-Jew, he is always a

[7]The rallying cry of Nazi storm troopers pursuing Jews in the streets.

Jew and it's always a special "Hep-Hep" that sounds in his ears. He can borrow someone else's mask, slip into someone else's skin, but the essential is elsewhere. The essential is that we remain Jews whatever transformation we may have undergone. There is something inside us, something that can't be put into words, a residue in the very depths of our soul—perhaps nothing more than an unconscious memory or a strange subterranean awareness, something we could never express but which we all feel, you, me, all the others, and which ceaselessly and continuously operates. Even if you abandon your Judaism, even if you want to cast it off as a snake sheds its skin, that ultimate residue will still be there inside you. And I can be as non-Jewish as you like, as blond inwardly as a *goy*, but the residue is in me just as much. In that respect we are totally equal.

And from the fact that we are Jews, and that any religious particularism is altogether extraneous, whether mine as it were from birth, or yours recently acquired, everything comes down to a question of attitude. And in this we differ, we find ourselves on two planes, this time with no link at all.

You know what you are doing and how to answer for it before your conscience. If you had to protect yourself, if it was necessary . . . but as it is, I can't understand you. No doubt I'm too young. I can't enter into your thoughts nor into this type of "prudence". Forgive me, Mother, I ask your forgiveness a thousand times, you know me, I'm quite different, and why not tell you that I'm terribly distressed that you've done this. It has happened so unexpectedly and I had never envisaged such a possibility. Which is why I've delayed so long in answering your letter. I've done a lot of thinking, started to write several times, hoping that eventually I would find an explanation that would shed light on you in my eyes. But I've found nothing.

I just can't understand you. But whatever I say and whatever you think, one thing remains. You can be the world's most fervent Catholic, you can execrate your Jewish blood, you can detest all things Jewish, but one thing remains. Unless you succeed in tearing everything away from yourself and ceasing to be one. But *to be* one, and yet *to say,* no, I'm not one—I'm sorry, it just won't do.

It's possible, Mother, that I shouldn't write to you like this. But you have been too frank with me for me not to know that it's not just a superficial formality with you, but that it's deep, very deep, to the point of rejection. I could have wished, wished with all my heart, that you'd not been so frank. You can tell me that I'm blinkered and chauvinistic, you can treat me as a Don Quixote, but, don't you see, one can believe oneself to be above all rules, to be a Fouché or a Mephistopheles, one can deny God and the world (I personally deny much more than you — religion and fatherland), and yet an Absolute exists that depends neither on our consent nor our denial, an Absolute where words no longer signify, where pride and personal honour are wishy-washy notions because they strut and swagger like shop-walkers—look, look, what a fine fellow I am! An Absolute that constitutes our innermost being and the very core of this being, which eludes our judgment and understanding, which is *given* like our life, like the world, primordial realities for us, unassailable and inexpressible. And this Jewish proclamation of my being is for me and inside me the most *absolute* thing I could ever imagine and feel, just as outside me God, the divine, is not something which takes Yes or No for an answer, which can be shoved off merely with an "I believe" or an "I don't believe".

And this is why I can't go against myself, you see, and force myself to understand a human being in whom this sense is lacking, even if that human being is my mother. Given that all this is so clear to me, and that my reaction seems to me more natural than any behaviour of mine in the past, I find it inconceivable that anyone could even mention the possibility of choice.

You know what my attitude would be on this point where strangers are concerned. But you are my mother and I love you and shall never stop looking for an explanation. I don't want to believe what I would have to believe following from all that I have said, and I beg you, I really earnestly beg you, to give me an answer that will enable me to see things in a different light. At first I meant to say, let's not discuss it. But that is impossible. So please, please explain yourself—perhaps it's you who's right and I'm the fool, I could wish for nothing better—and if you can't explain yourself now, then say that you will later, when we next meet.

Perhaps you understand me rather better now. I didn't make my decision so as to become a different person (I know I'll never be a Jew in the way you imagine), nor so as to be useful to anyone nor even so as to fight (a Don Quixote, you say. But how? I'm not fighting). That's not the point; you're so wrong. I don't want to shed my skin, like you. I'm not adopting a new religion, I'm not changing course in midstream. *I am a Jew and I say so,* just as I have always done. Is that strange, is that new? With others, everyone knows that they're Jews and they don't need to publish the fact. But with me it isn't known, and this is why I have to proclaim it. These things go without saying, Mother, because, do what you will, you will never be able to suppress the fact that I have a Jewish mother. You say it may harm me if I don't hide what I am. Should I therefore think awry? What would be the sense in that? I wasn't faced with a choice that had to be made, I wasn't compelled to adopt a point of view. I did what was for me the most natural thing in the world, what went without saying. Inward clarity/outward clarity, challenge/response. One point, that's all. I've stayed the same, Mother, and that's what matters. And tell me, please, how could I possibly be one sometimes, and not be one at other times, and all solely for reasons of expediency?

And it's on this note that I shall finish: I belong to a group of people who lead a particular kind of life. It behooves them not to conceal this particularity, but rather to reveal it. There's no merit attached to it; it's simply a historical fact stretching over thousands of years. The nations can do what they like; they have the power and they make us feel it. We have to endure it, each in his own way. One thing only depends on us: the path along which we must pass, with our heads held high, in the consciousness of being not only marked out but honoured (an honour that should entail not pride, but duty) and . . . in humanity. The answer won't long be delayed. It will be given one day, perhaps by many, perhaps by only very few among us.

As for Uncle Schr, he finished his letter with the ominous phrase, "My decision is irrevocable." What decision, in heaven's name? Did the "Old Man"[8] seriously think I would ever go back to Germany? And so I too remain unshakable. If I still had to thank him for something or other, it's now done.

And now, dearest, let me remind you of your promise to send me a photograph of you. I wish you all much happiness, and you personally so many good things . . . and stand fast! And no more stories about depression, do you hear? I kiss you with all my love,

Your Peter

[8]The pet name that Peter's mother had given to her husband, Erich Schrobsdorff.

Faro, 18 February 1939

Dear Mother,

Once again you haven't understood me and haven't realised what I'm after. Strange! You always pride yourself on being such a good psychologist! This time your psychology is at fault so I must speak more plainly. It appears that I'm not sufficiently alone even now—there are still too many people meddling in my affairs without being asked. What I want is to be forgotten. I want to be free, do you understand? So free that my life and actions belong only to myself and won't be endlessly discussed, criticised, approved of, censured. People can chatter away as much as they like, but let them leave me in peace. Above all, don't imagine that I mind their opinion of me, good God no! I couldn't care less what they think, what any of them think: Uncle Schr, Father, Enie[9], Aunt Lucy, the lot. Their advice irritates me, so do their letters; it's always the same thing. I haven't the slightest desire to explain my position. Just tell me this: By what right do they interfere in my affairs and tell me lies about my life and what I ought to be doing? What do they know about what I ought to be doing? I'm not in the least cross, I'm just amazed at the vast "wisdom" of these people.

Perhaps even you haven't yet grasped my point: I don't want to have anything more to do with them, not because they don't understand me—that's of no importance whatever—but because I'm not interested in making myself understood. I don't want to get any more letters or write them. They're living their life and I'm living mine. What concern is it of theirs whether I'm working, whether I've got "plans", whether I'm living

[9]Enie, Peter's father's second wife.

as a crook or a beggar? Their phrase—"We only want your good"—it makes me puke. Do you know what my dream is? To find a place where no one knows me, where there's no post office, where I'm completely alone. Not to hear anyone talked about, not to know about anyone else and even to be forgotten—forgotten for good or only seemingly so. Not to say anything, not to explain anything, to do what the moment dictates. To live according to my mood, like this today, like that tomorrow, without yesterday or tomorrow, without links or obligations, without plans or projects for the future—to live, to live. No useless baggage, no memories, no points of reference. To feel free, without possessing anything, without being possessed, a tramp like Villon, like Rimbaud. To live with the day, with the night, to live and be constantly awake, to live and write . . .

Yes, I'd like to be Rimbaud, to go to Africa or any other unknown country far away; to live there and forget all about the vacuities, absurdities, inferiorities, presumptions, complacencies great or small, the whole pompous edifice based on lying, self-esteem, convention, meanness, pettiness, violence, and crime that is called Europe, that sophisticated piece of machinery that kills and slaughters with every turn of the wheel, and each of whose parts—call it society, city, state, civilization or anything else—is an abyss of falsehood and bankruptcy, nothing but a corpse because they've murdered the last hope within it. I want to forget all that, as Rimbaud did; I don't want to know about it. I would like to say with him: *Je regrette l'Europe,* because life, the world, and truth are elsewhere and because I'm lucky enough to know it and take action in consequence . . . Portugal is no more than a lamentable compromise.

I'm alarming you perhaps and you're going to accuse me of selfishness again. And perhaps you're right, because in other times I would have left you one fine day, both of you, you understand, you and Liena, after a last look and without turning round. And I would have gone far, much farther than I came five months ago, and you would never have heard of me again. Or I would have gone now, after a time of trial, and probably still farther and more secretly. But I would always have freed myself with the same consequence and nothing could have held me back. For the desire for freedom would have been stronger, stronger than love and the community; stronger than anything, I feel it.

But today all that's a dream. The constellation is different, even in me. I neither can nor want to leave you. Something stronger than ourselves and even our wildest desires binds us together. We must always be there for each other's sake, ready at any moment to turn round and do what we can. I have realised this and am organizing myself accordingly. So the union with you both is quite natural.

That all this has nothing to do with love is obvious. Just as the desire to break away does not stem from a lack of love, so today's unconditional union is not caused by a surplus of love. The emotion is always the same, and who could love you more than I do, and by whom could Liena be loved more than by me? No, this aspiration towards freedom (which does not exclude a deep and sincere love, for I would have come back one day) and towards true isolation (what is my present one?), this selfishness if you like, is a requirement within me and has its source somewhere else. But there's no question of my not renouncing a little of this freedom. Except for you two and a few others, I have gone away irrevocably and shall never return. The others can forget me, they can go to hell. Have I made myself clear? You tell me I hurt people. But this simply doesn't matter to me. If they can't bear the simple truth, that's their affair. My links with them no longer have any value for me. So it hasn't the slightest importance whether I break them or not. Breaking is easier. It's childish of you to argue that this will harm me. I no longer live in their universe, so there's no need for me to take my cue from them. I'm doing things that I regard as right and I don't want others to criticise them, for they concern no one but me. I don't depend on anyone, I can stand on my own feet, what more do you want?

But on one point I can put your heart at rest: These thoughts have certainly not come to me because I'm poor or unhappy or think I'm "on the wrong tack" (oh Mother . . .). Everything is going to my greatest satisfaction and I'm doing excellently. I'm being absolutely honest and not telling lies; you needn't have the slightest worry about me or my future. You know what my activities are. You'll know more about them later. I'm only just starting.

You've been a very bad psychologist in all this, Mother dear. What you call arrogance is simply a desire not to be pestered any more. It's self-defence, not distress, that's all.

As for your advice that I should go back on my decision, it strikes a completely false note after my last letter.

Take care of yourself, Mother, and answer quickly. And don't worry, all will be well. It's my grandparents who are having to endure the most, but not for long I hope. Kiss them a thousand times for me. I love them so much.

Do come here, it would be marvellous, and the best and healthiest thing that the earth could give you at the moment. You'd store up strength for years, and you'd arrive at just the right season and have your beloved sun from morning till night. And I'm sure we'd manage to explain ourselves to each other on various points—which is not without its importance.

How delighted I would be, imagine it! Give my love to the children and a thousand loving wishes to you, and a big hug.

Your Peter

Have you seen Liena by any chance?

Faro, 2 March 1939

Dearest Mother,

You haven't written to me and I've been so longing for your letter. If you were offended now it really would be grotesque. I've great news: I'm working! In a firm that exports sardines. I'm in charge of the English, German, and French correspondence. Where the last language is concerned more or less "on faith". But that doesn't matter. I started at the beginning of the month and am getting four hundred escudos for the first two trial months. It's not a lot but it's more than I need. After the trial period we shall make a new arrangement to our mutual satisfaction. The boss is a nice man and has taken a great fancy to me—so far; I shall soon be promoted to being a representative. Hours of work: from half past nine to twelve and from two to six.

So I now belong to the commercial scene. I may yet discover I've got a bump for trade. Probably not, but I'm getting used to surprises.

Besides which, I'm giving a few lessons and my life is as it were transformed. But it's nothing really special.

If you write to me, could you tell me whether you've made up your mind to come here? You'd only have the fares to pay and they aren't very expensive.

Dearest Mother, let me go on having this illusion: I'm confidently expecting you.

I love you.

Your Peter

Kiss all the others!

Faro, 19 March 1939

Mother darling,

News from you at last. I'd been waiting and waiting! A thousand thanks for your two letters, a thousand thanks for your explanations, a thousand thanks for your final words—it's good, it's right, there's nothing bad in it.

And now we won't discuss it any more—at least not by letter. I understand now how things developed within you until they became a necessity, and all my fears have now vanished. I realise that you had to arrive at that point. The fact that I would have been incapable of it myself is neither here nor there. But why should we suppose that we're exactly alike?

The essential thing is that your decision, which certainly wasn't an easy one for you to make (as at first I feared it was, because I couldn't interpret your words otherwise—I know now that there was no cynicism on your part), is fully justified by the fact that you have become a believer.

In this respect I can't pretend to follow you through to the end. Because the essence of religion, namely adoration, is completely foreign to me. That the divine exists is obvious; it doesn't even admit of discussion, it's a primordial truth encompassing all the meaning and all the beauty of the world. But the relationship with God, the distance between the human and the divine — if we want to speak figuratively — is the infinite variable which we are always trying to determine. And for me religion has no value because it is a mediation that distances rather than brings near; indeed it has so many images and laws outside the immediate divine that it would take a whole lifetime to learn them and understand them. Thus religion becomes an end in itself, and this at once robs it of any *raison d'être*.

In my opinion there is no institution that has created so many difficulties as the Church regarding man's need to go to God, in other words to live with him and in him, to be as close to him or far from him as to one's own innermost life. A society that preaches God's anger and the fear one should feel before him is, in my view, a society incapable of saying — if only summarily — what the divine is. And when this society wants to celebrate his love and prove it, it is still more removed from his essence, if this is possible. For God is one of those strange beings who do not love but can only be loved.

But what I have just said is not really of capital importance. In the final analysis what we believe doesn't matter much. What matters is that things should acquire a meaning only if they have a centre. Something by which the significance we attach to them equals our obligations towards them. That's all we really need. You believe—that's fine! You have found a teaching that gives you peace and serenity. You are detached from the things of here below — that's splendid! You have met a Father John—you admire him and you've become humble. What unexpected outcomes!

No, there's nothing bad in it. But that's no reason why you should disown, and this you won't do. I knew you wouldn't. Because that's the second essential point: the "general question". It's something altogether independent of your faith and your aversion to Judaism. No one wants you to experience joy where you don't experience it and to love what you don't love. There is nevertheless a loyalty that we must observe at all costs. It is our highest duty and that goes for you too. There is the absolutely elementary fact of being beaten and the obligation to respond—and there is also the beautiful word "brotherhood". This word says nothing to you in this context, you feel nothing—fair enough, there's nothing to be done about that, because people are different. But one certainly has a right to ask you for loyalty.

As for your two epithets—"proclamation" and "display"—they are caricatures of my thought and I want to tell you this: There are times in life when we are obliged not only to see things clearly but to state them clearly. You no doubt forget that marriage and a blessing are also "proclamations". You also forget that I didn't want to expound my point of view at the Consulate. All I wanted to do was to make use of the means at my disposal to put an end to a "legal" distinction—which was only right. Moreover, I don't think I'm behaving altogether mistakenly if I can show by my example what a Jew is, or perhaps what a Jew *also* is, at a time when only vileness is law.

What you say about "my country" falls absolutely flat. It is not my country, and never will be. I owe Germany nothing but my mother tongue—which is, I admit, a lot, and the only thing which I am able or willing to preserve. So if you can approve my decision, because it is necessary, as I can yours, because it is necessary to you, we shall at any rate have obtained unconditional respect for our opposing goals.

Let me repeat that I understand you and that I no longer hold anything against you. If there's anything further to say about it then we can discuss it when we meet and put an end to the question.

What a glorious hope that is! Will you come? Oh please, please do. You can't begin to imagine how much I long to see you. I can't really think about anything else.

And do rest assured that the tide will soon turn. You mustn't take too black a view of things, all will change.

I don't really know what I ought to say about Dimiter. Events come crowding in and any conventional congratulations would be absurd. Naturally my ardent wish is that this union will bring you nothing but happiness. I've never met him, which is why we shall wait a little. I shall always be a friend to him.

There's one thing in your letter that astonished me: You're celebrating something. What's it all about—celebrating? What are you celebrating? I just can't remember what on earth it can be.

Please do go and see Liena and Tatiana.[10] It's a long time since I heard from Liena. I have no idea what's happening. It makes me very sad that she doesn't write, and I'm frightened. I love her as much as ever, even more. She is my only woman. From the moment I first got to know her I've never given a thought to anyone else, and ever since I left Germany I've been what is called faithful to her. With complete freedom, without doing any violence to myself.

And now, Mother dear, you mustn't be distressed. We're always together. I see that now more clearly than ever before. Oh how I long to talk to you!

As for me, I'm well though perhaps a little tired. My cat, Ariel, is a source of indescribable joy. Last

[10]Liena was the daughter of the Russian ballerina Tatiana Gsovsky.

Sunday I went to the sea for the first time and it was gorgeous.

All my love, my little Mother . . . and as you know, I'm waiting for you to come. I kiss you a thousand times.

Always your Peter

My love to the grandparents and the children. I shall write to Uncle Schr.

Faro, 5 April 1939

Dear Mother,

My best wishes to all of you for Easter and Pesach.[11]

If you go to the Russian church you'll meet Liena and Tatiana. Unfortunately I know nothing about what's happening to you all, but it gets boring to be always asking the same questions.

Again you're not writing—it's nearly three weeks now since I received a letter. Not to mention the silence you insisted on keeping before that. So be it!

As for Liena, she's not written for two months. That she too should have found something nearer to hand was predictable. I can't do anything about that either, much as I would like to. It's depressing that so few people can face a hardship for the love of others who themselves are having to face an equal or more cruel one.

I haven't loved very much in my life so far. Twice. But the twice that I've given myself entirely, and as if it were for ever, I've done so with all the love and generos-

[11]Passover.

ity I was capable of, without reserve, without counting the cost, and never have I received more than a tiny fraction of what I gave. This wouldn't be serious in itself if she had been able to rise above the greatest—indeed the only—real hardship. But it's depressing to discover that separation inevitably brings with it the end of love.

Thank my grandparents for their two letters which I intend to answer just as soon as I've a little more time. Take care of yourself. I kiss you.

Peter

Faro, 26 April 1939

Darling Mother,

Many thanks for your two letters, the photographs, and the grammars—which you shouldn't have bought new. I haven't answered till today because your last letter, the one with the Bulgarian address, was at the post office for five days without my knowing.[12]

Your letter frightened me. And so you've got out, that's obvious. Where will it stop? I'm clinging to the hope that the days that followed the posting of this SOS were easier for you, and that your distress was primarily due to the journey, the separations, the novelty, the unknown. I understand your misgivings and your depression better than anyone. And I am so close to you that it's unthinkable that you shouldn't feel it. But you must wait, Mother, and get a little bit calm. It's no good

[12]Peter's mother emigrated to Bulgaria in April, 1939. Her two daughters remained in Berlin. They joined her—one at a time so as not to attract attention—a little later.

wanting to understand everything all at once. No one can explain everything to you. You must let a little while pass without thinking about anything—just let things be — and anyway how do you know things are going against you? Who is telling you that they're not going in your favour and are not taking care of you — you who have arrived so totally unprovided for? You must show a little patience, just a little. I know it's difficult and that you're thoroughly disoriented, but you have no other choice. Is there ever a period in our life when we don't have to give proof of patience? I experience this every day and in sufferings for which I'm grateful; patience is everything.

Liena has written, and what I foresaw has indeed happened. For her this is quite natural, she had to follow this path. One day she will perhaps realise that there are more important things than surrendering everything to love on the pretext that it's too strong to resist.

But, as you rightly point out, this experience is not of great importance to me. Not only is it not new, but I was absolutely certain that I would have to go through it a second time. It couldn't have been otherwise and I was in full knowledge of the facts when I departed. And this although she was my greatest love. Today I have been in a certain sense set free, for when all is said and done I was giving myself not so much to Liena as to love. Do you understand what I mean? And Liena couldn't take love from me, for my love was not only for her but for many other things too. Consequently I'm absolutely calm and in fact not much has changed. So we won't talk about it any more.

Now, Mother, would it be a good idea if I came to live with you? What do you think? My longing to see you has never been so great. We could go forward side by side, couldn't we, and be stronger together? Couldn't we live together, live solely for each other? How I should love to live only for you! Don't you think we could both begin a new life—I mean, new between you and me? I feel that I could be much closer to you than I am to myself.

Think about it very seriously. I'd come and you'd no longer be alone; we'd live together and work together if possible. If not, we'd work on our own. And you would have a son and a friend, I would be with you and if you wanted to cry I wouldn't let you.

I'm fully aware that I'd have to give up many things if I came to you, on the other hand I now realise that I absolutely must come live with you if you don't come to me. It's impossible for me to have peace unless I know that peace has returned to you.

What is certain is that you won't make me change my mind. I shall become a Jew. That's decided. Henceforth you can only approve or disapprove. My wishes for Pesach weren't addressed to you but to my grandparents. Don't think that I'm going to torment you by saying again what I've said before. I'm sorry that my words could have given grounds for such an interpretation. As regards Bettina, you won't be able to keep it from her — she'll know the truth one day.[13] But let's leave that for the moment.

Write to me quickly. And don't lose courage. And please tell me everything that happens to you. My love for you is infinite, as always. Millions of kisses.

Your Peter

[13]The two daughters did not know that their mother was Jewish. See the letter to Bruno Kirschner of 1 April 1940, p. 154.

Faro, 5 May 1939

My dearest Mother,

You can imagine what incredible delight today's letter from you has given me. A very different story from two weeks ago! Calm and happy! You've taken an immense weight from my mind. I had been so afraid for you. I thought you wouldn't be able to pull through by yourself. Good, so all is now more or less in order and you will see your doubts and fears disappearing as you get more accustomed to your new life; soon you will feel that you've never lived anywhere else but Bulgaria. And soon you'll go to Varna, and you'll have the children with you again and also the "Old Man", and what more could you want? My dear one, my sweet one, it's all like a comedy, like a puppet-show. Reunions, joy, life together, separation, farewells, sorrow, then reunions again—just like clockwork.

I've heaps of questions to ask you and you absolutely must answer them, whether clearly or not. Why in fact did you not come here? First you wrote that we would see each other soon, then that there were no more difficulties "now"—and I was happier than I'd ever been before (quite apart from the important fact that we had to explain so many things to each other)—and then—I'm in Sofia. Just that, without comment, as if it were the most natural thing in the world. I really don't understand you. I quite agree that, at the moment, we have to give up pleasure trips because I don't imagine either of us has the money for that. So the question is very simple: Do you want to have me with you? Can I be of any practical use to you? And is there any possibility of entering Bulgaria as a German Jew? Mind you answer these questions. Are you unwilling or unable to have me, or is it simply preferable that I shouldn't come? Let me know.

This is what happens when everyone goes his own way. I don't know whether you're working, how things stand with the children, or what the situation is in general. I know absolutely nothing. Please do give me as clear and detailed an account of events as you can; I really want to be in the know. Is this asking too much? As for me, I shall now tell you how *I* live.

I get up between eight and nine o'clock, say good-morning to Ariel and out we go together to greet the six little pigs, the two little goats, a dog, Nero, as ugly as he is amiable, and a whole farmyard that besieges me as Hannibal did poor Rome. Then I swallow a cup of what Rosaria calls coffee, together with two slices of bread and margarine. That's my breakfast and it never varies. It's already a long time since I forgot the taste of butter.

The day having started, I find myself faced with a very difficult choice: Whether to go to the office at ten or eleven. (In the past—that is to say before 1 May—things were quite different, as I had to arrive at half past nine, work until twelve, kill as best I could the two hours' break for lunch and then work again till six or later.) But on the first of May I let my boss know that the two hours' break in the middle of the day was absolutely unacceptable as far as I was concerned, that I could gulp down my meal in ten minutes, and that the break interrupted my day in a thoroughly tiresome way. He accepted this and so it was agreed that I would cut down the famous break to half an hour and start work either at ten in the morning and finish at five in the afternoon, or at eleven and finish at six. So I have a little free time which at the moment I use for writing letters, but soon I shall take advantage of it, if the

Portuguese spring permits (more about that spring later), to go to the sea — either in the morning or the evening.

At the office (there are three of us plus an errand boy) I am a prop and pillar to my boss. Though engaged as translator for the foreign correspondence, I'm occupied almost exclusively with Portuguese (I write letters which I submit to the boss for correction before I type them). From time to time a letter arrives in English or German. I should have mentioned that my boss is absolutely mad about organization; every day he enacts new "rules" and behaves as if he's got at least a hundred people under his orders. And so I've got a "Department" all to myself. I won't go into details, for, as far as sardines, anchovies, the shapes and sizes of preserving-tins, advertising, bills, commissions, and exports go — in short everything to do with this commercial activity of primary importance — you know as little as I once did. Let me say only this — that Moroccan competition just doesn't exist, because *our* sardines are so much fatter! And as for poor quality oil, well that doesn't really matter much. The essential thing is "organization"—and the fact that "in the Portuguese tinned fish industry, our firm is reputed to be one of the best" (my boss's favourite sentence).

There. So I work flat out for about six and a half hours to keep our "reputation" at pitch point. The boss is kind and cultivated, which is rare here. Sometimes he invites me to his home. He has six children: three sweet little girls, two boys of fifteen and sixteen (who aren't allowed on the simplest excursion, for fear they might drink unfiltered water on the way), and an older daughter who spends her time trying to get married. His wife is ravishing, but he is unfaithful to her, as is the custom. The whole family lives in a horrible house; however, they have a much larger and nicer villa on the outskirts. But it would take the mother and daughter *ten minutes* to get to the centre from there. Just imagine!

To return to me. At twelve I go to the post-office, then to the newspaper kiosk (it's cheaper). When work is over I take the bus back to Marina where Ariel and Nero are waiting for me. I pull an easy chair out onto my flowery verandah and do anything or nothing. At half past seven I begin to argue with Rosaria about the possibility of dining before nine, and this sometimes happens, when she's in a good mood.

You will have noticed that I no longer have a woman to clean for me. Not since December. I do the cleaning myself on Sundays and sometimes, very rarely, Carmo comes and does my washing. I'm on very good terms with her, we're always helping each other out, and we don't pay the slightest attention to the malicious gossip our relationship arouses. But my favourite is her daughter Sarah; she has recently had measles and, to cheer her up, I gave her a dress that has thrown the whole family into perplexity as to my good taste. I've lost all credit in this domain anyway since introducing into my room a photograph of a naked man from the Sistine Chapel and some "death's heads" (that's what Carmo calls my photographs of Verlaine and Rilke and a reproduction of Queen Nefertiti).

Nearly every day I give English lessons from eight to nine in the evening. After which I go to bed and read. Stendhal's *The Red and the Black*, Goethe's *Apprenticeship of Wilhelm Meister*, de Coster's *Eulenspiegel* and *Leonardo da Vinci* by Merezhkovsky are my most recent reading. From time to time I dip into some history of literature, then *Faust* and *Hamlet*, but not to the end. In a disorderly way, higgledy-piggledy. I've read and reread Rimbaud's fine poems, didn't really understand *Saison en enfer* and *Illuminations*, I mean

I'm not capable of rising to such heights. Rilke very seldom, but always with the same delight. I can't understand people not liking him. He's one of those pure poets of whom there aren't many. To go to him in a secular frame of mind is impossible.

I've hardly done any writing since 1 March. It's sad and every day I reproach myself for it. But I can't force myself when I'm tired. And that's my trouble: I'm often very tired. Everything requires effort and I need a lot of sleep — in this I'm my father's son. If it happens that I'm still awake at one o'clock in the morning I feel it very keenly the next day. It's ridiculous really because I'm in good health and in fact I'm extremely well. The devil alone knows what makes me incapable of doing anything at all after a certain hour at night. Yet it's unfortunately true; there are Balzac and the others.

As usual I'm more or less alone and haven't any real companion. Now and again a young man from Olhao visits me in the evening, or I go see him. We chat until late at night and, when I go see him, we sometimes listen to music on the radio. He isn't very interesting but he's kind and obliging. He works at the town hall where he has my affairs in hand and docs all hc can to help me; so our friendship is valuable to me from the practical point of view. I am in fact on very good terms with all the administration and am allowed to come and go as I will even in the holiest of holies. That's a great quality of the Portuguese: They are always friendly and prepared to do one a service. Never once has anyone been rude to me. If only I could say that of the Germans! If ever a Portuguese is discourteous, it's not through ill-will, but thoughtlessness.

Their eternal remark when they address me is, "But you speak Portuguese so well already." Indeed I do speak it fairly fluently, though my vocabulary is very limited and I'm not yet able to express what I want to say when the conversation is on a high level. Portuguese constructions are very special and cause enormous worry to anyone lacking a deep knowledge of the language. But it's a beautiful language and it makes you lose the taste for Spanish—though you can't bear to admit it at first. You get used to its gentle modulations so quickly that the hard Spanish consonants come to seem forced, exactly like Dutch to us Germans. In fact I'm incapable of saying a single sentence in Spanish now, though I read it easily, a facility which the resemblance between the two languages makes possible while making it impossible to speak the other. A pity!

You want to know what I'm earning. Well, I've moved on from four to six hundred escudos, that is as much as the accountant and more than my friend in the town hall. It's rare here to pay salaries higher than six hundred escudos, so I've nothing to complain of.

And finally, the climate. When you speak of the heat and of going swimming I can only roar with laughter. First of all, I have never in my life been so cold as during this winter. Secondly, I have never longed so impatiently for spring. Thirdly, I have never been so deceived. It's really lamentable. Of course there have been one or two warm days when we said: At last! Yes, well, believe it or not, there's no at last at all, and no spring and no South and no "sunny country without a winter"! It's a real hoax, the South! I've only been in the water twice since October. The first time was lovely and hot and that was in March. The second was four days ago and it was freezing. No matter who I talk to I'm assured that it's absolutely exceptional and that other years, yes, other years . . . I can only say, so that's how it is; I arrive in Portugal and the climate is no longer what it was — bad luck. When they talk about summer and say, just wait and you'll see, I laugh derisively—you can't bluff me any more, you scoundrels! Go to the devil with your South! And here's me, poor innocent, who at first didn't even want to bring my winter overcoat!

I'll finish now, Mother dearest, for this has again become an interminable letter. How I do write! And you, just two meagre little pages. Answer this quickly. I long to hear from you. And don't let's talk about Jewishness any more. You can't change anything. Each person does what he must. And with regard to help, let's wait, we'll see.

All my love to the children, to the grandparents and to Uncle Schr (I thought he was going to write to me).

And you I kiss a thousand times and am

Your Peter

I could, of course, write another 283 pages, talk to you about myself and all sorts of other things. And yet nothing has happened and every day is the same. But is there a single day that isn't infinitely rich in events if we look at it closely enough?

Faro, 31 May 1939

My dearest Mother,

If only you knew the joy and happiness your letters give me, although they could hardly be called cheering! But I've often said before and shall never tire of repeating, I'm so close to you, Mother, and I think only of you, always. Then when you talk to me I'm happy and possessed with the one desire to be with you. I miss you so much! And if you say again that I don't think well of you, if you attribute my delay in writing to that sort of nonsense, then I'll get very cross. You must never make suppositions like that, never, do you understand?

I always think about you in the same way and you couldn't possibly wish for a better.

When I think over what you've written to me I always come to the same conclusion: We must try very hard to join each other and then stay together. I see no other solution for casting out your wild misgivings and convincing you that what you've done is right.

You're not really capable of living alone, and so you oughtn't to be doing it. Not only because you're a woman, but also because there's no earthly need, no earthly reason, internal or external, which compels you to adopt a life of solitude. You don't want to, and you're perfectly right not to want to, so we must try to change what can be changed. It's difficult but not beyond our reach provided we have a firm will and a steadfast intention.

And this is why all that I shall undertake in the future will have one sole purpose: to build up a life together at no matter what price. I shan't do anything more just for myself, but only for *us*. I shall try everything in my power. How, where and when you mustn't ask me just now. I can only give you this assurance: You have my utterly unconditional help and my efforts will never waver. For your good first and foremost, but just as much for the good of both of us. Dearest Mother, you must be patient, patient with me, patient with yourself, patient with others, and you must stop complaining, stop thinking you are to blame, stop inveighing against men and destiny. You must accept the facts as they are and not as catastrophic upheavals. Which in any case they are not. You are ungrateful, Mother, and you don't realise how lucky you are not to have to live in Germany, in that wasteland, that intellectual morass, much more evil than the worst of violence and so dangerous that it poisons even reasonable men who, after a sufficient amount of "conditioning", are tempted to follow their model and rate high what is low and lose sight of the eternal human values. It is sad, infinitely sad, that a man like my father should spend his life writing plays for the people. It will always be a mystery to me how cultivated men can endure it and don't do all in their power to escape from that prison and exchange a guaranteed livelihood (relative though it is) for intellectual freedom and some form of human responsibility. But we shall leave that, because in your opinion I'm prejudiced; please God that others may have my prejudice, then perhaps we'll be able to get something done.

And then I'd like to answer you with your own words: Think of all the people, all the Jews, who are much worse off than you, who are hungry and don't even know where to lay their heads. Who haven't seen their children for years. Whose loved ones are perhaps dead or in the hands of the torturers. You're ungrateful, Mother!

And if you say that you have created your own unhappiness and should never have emigrated, then try to imagine exactly what the alternative would have been. What would have happened?

No, no, my dearest Mother, I know everything, I take account of everything, and I also understand you very well. It is hard for you, harder than for many others, and yet infinitely less hard than might have been feared. And you mustn't forget that. Nor that we are living according to new arrangements and that the old ones are no longer appropriate. That too is a fact.

And then you mustn't allow your doubts about yourself to work themselves up into an inferiority complex. It's utterly ridiculous. It is obvious that in a situation like yours you are not in a position to take on anything new. In order to do that you would first have to become free and rediscover that confidence which alone brings stability. But you're sailing with a strong list. Which means that you need help and there's only one thing for you to do: accept this help and don't make it too difficult. And in this way all reflections on your incapacity become superfluous. I'm convinced that if you had someone beside you who was urging you to start work, you would find all the strength, energy and skill you need to bring any task you might choose to a successful conclusion.

So please try to pull yourself together enough to be able to say when the decisive moment comes: Here I am, what's to be done? Get rid of everything that weighs you down, and hope with me. You'll have your children with you soon and perhaps with God's help we'll manage to free my grandparents. Have patience!

I don't really know about the situation in Bulgaria, though I had always assumed that from the political point of view it wasn't exactly wise to go to the East which is more or less, as you yourself say, under German influence. But as you seem to look on Bulgaria as only a stepping stone, it isn't impossible that between now and your departure the situation will remain unchanged. Do please let me know at once about your intentions and about all the arrangements you may make regarding them. You can't go on making decisions without consulting me, you can't just present me with accomplished facts. Let me repeat for the hundredth time: A permanent contact between us is indispensable.

My deliberations and proposals with a view to emigrating to Bulgaria thus no longer hold good for they were based on false premises. In a general way, when you say that I don't really visualize the reality, I can only answer: You purposely omitted to give me the necessary information. Meanwhile, I have more or less got to know the facts. Finally, I still hope to ascertain on what money you're living. Please give me a detailed answer.

Today is Liena's birthday, and it's now exactly a year since we exchanged "rings". What moonshine! I've already moved very far from all that, and it's only now and again . . . but that doesn't matter any more. What did happen still lives.

My darling little Mother, hold on and don't judge things wrong. You still have a lot in front of you. A day will come when you won't understand yourself any more. And believe me we two, you and me, you understand, shall come through. Be calm and know that I shall do everything for you and that I love you more than the whole world. And salvation, interior salvation, always comes only from within ourselves.

Your Peter

Faro, 8 June 1939

Dearest Mother,

Are you still as unhappy as you were? When are the children arriving? Today is Tina's[14] birthday and let's hope she is happy. Here there have been various changes. We have had a lot of comings and goings in the house—Jews and *goyim* galore. Recently a little Swiss man arrived who wanted to convert me to Protestantism. When I told him I was a Protestant he seemed disappointed. Yet he talked a great deal about God and about his own life, dear little man. But, you see, these Sunday afternoon conversations on lofty sub-

[14]Bettina.

jects, when you're thinking about totally different things and haven't the faintest desire to make your beliefs known, but feel you have to say something because a little man is sitting there who wants to expatiate on everything he's learnt, well frankly I can't take it all with due courtesy. To cut a long story short—and how we got bogged down in it I don't really know—I read him Faust's gorgeous dialogue about God, and the little man found it very interesting and pounced on the book with a genuine desire to learn and to verify whether Goethe had said something really Christian here or there which a little man like he could latch onto with good reason. But having discovered nothing he took his leave, with renewed assurances that "it really was worthwhile to have read it."

A German-Jewish family from Lisbon has recently settled in here. It is distinguished by an exceptionally pretty pair of twins who are adored by their father (barely two-and-a-half years old, with fiery red hair); a kind, lively, rather flighty wife; and one of those semi-cultivated Jewish businessmen who know everything about everything and jump from one thing to another and yet are by no means stupid. They invite me to join them from time to time and it's very agreeable because we converse with great ease. They're very affable in any case, in addition to being Jews (whom I always understand, however peculiar they may be). But these ones aren't at all peculiar and they have a splendid African earthenware jar in their room which makes up for a great deal. Their name is Berthoff.

The Portuguese can be terribly disillusioning. There's a boy who works in the town hall who comes to visit me every Sunday and bores me to tears. I didn't know how to convey this to him, but now there'll be no problem! Because last Sunday, not content with having inflicted his presence on me for a whole afternoon (I was making valiant efforts to conceal my boredom and rejoicing at the thought that I would soon be alone again), he suddenly realised when night fell that it was getting late, that the sky was dark, that he would have difficulty getting home, and that it would be preferable to stay the night with me. In my innocence I said, "Of course, here's my bed, make yourself at home, but if you don't mind I'll sleep in it too as I haven't another one." At first all went well, until, finally, well, he became importunate. It was a pretty disturbed night as I had to be on my guard the whole time against the good man's advances. Moreover my boss has also been somewhat disillusioning. At first I took him for an absolutely reasonable man, but since he bought a book entitled *How I Became A Strong Person,* and leaves it lying about for days on end on his desk without understanding it, since then I've given up.

One consolation has been the visit of our American agent, Snr. Calderon (a Spaniard) who talked to me in German as if he'd done nothing else all his life. If I'm not mistaken he too is a Jew and Feliciano, my boss, is of the same opinion. In any case it would be surprising if he weren't. I could also tell you about a Bavarian called Stichhauer Roth and a gentleman from Faro who limps along and whenever he meets me gives me a detailed account of his physical ills and those of his wife—the refrain is: "I got a bullet in my head during the war"... but that really would involve too great a digression.

Next Sunday I'm invited to a wedding and it will be dreadfully jolly. God, how liberated we are.

Oh, and I miss music terribly! If only I could listen to a concert. Do you know I'd start studying music even now if I could. Absolutely seriously. It's ridiculous anyway to be so ignorant. I ought to study history, the history of art, philosophy. So many things I ought to do. Life is organized so wisely that everything in it has its seem long again to me one day! You said a very beautiful thing in one of your letters: "God is a great artist. Life is organized so wisely that everything in it has its compensation, and finally death itself will seem so close one day that you will not feel it as difficult, but as something good and necessary." I'm sure you're right, though I personally can't yet envisage a time when I shall cease to hate and fear death. I'm terribly afraid of it, I must admit, and I think it's a huge sin that men should gamble their lives in war, in suicide, or simply through carelessness. For this life has been given them for fulfilment in its own terms, however hard it may be, and not with a view to another. Each life has as its goal to produce something living, something autonomous, and that is why the artistic life seems to me the truest and the most justified, for it leaves behind—in the purest, most valid and most manifest way—something that endures or at least strives to do so.

I long for an answer from you, my dearest, and I'm always thinking of you. Take care of yourself, and may everything turn out for the best for you in Varna. Goodbye my . . . my woman, and try not to worry. This is my hourly prayer. I kiss you.

Your Peter

Faro, 26 June 1939

Darling Mother,

What special thing should I wish for you on your birthday? I'm afraid of becoming unbearably repetitive, because everything I've got to say to you I've said already in one form or another: whether wishes, longings, hopes. So how can I highlight this particular day in the way that custom requires? Should I say that I'm thinking about you with my whole strength? But I've only one way of thinking about you. Or that I'm dying with longing to see you? But this longing never leaves me. Or that I would like to give you all that's best in the world and to know that you're calm and smiling? But you know full well that this is my only wish. Or that I love you and that you are first and foremost in my life? But you know this too. So what can I say to make this day stand out from others on which you already have the first of my thoughts? And how could today's thoughts and wishes be more tender than usual, since every day and every hour I give you my fondest love? So you see it's not easy for me to enshrine this date with a special halo. For me it's your birthday every day and that's the present I give you.

Many thanks for your letter which again had been long awaited. All seems to be well; you're getting used to things, you're more cheerful, you don't feel so generally oppressed. I'm glad that you're meeting people, that you're regaining your eye for beauty, that you're gradually becoming the good old "Schnuff"![15] A letter like this makes me so happy! Go on along these lines, Mother, and soon you'll have forgotten why you ever regretted emigration. And how about the children and my grandparents? We'll find a solution, all will be possible. A little time, a little patience.

As for what you tell me about the children and their life in Germany, I entirely endorse what you say.

[15]The pet name that Peter as a child had given his mother and that all her friends had adopted in speaking of her.

They're becoming thoroughly spoiled and are losing all sense of judgment. And that's what we should at least preserve. All the joy and love they're receiving counts as nothing by comparison. It is bad, it is suspect, it is dangerous in the highest degree to be happy in Germany. There's tribulation in Germany, and this is how it ought to be and this is how it's right to be. We must change our ways of thinking, we must be partisans, under pain of losing ourselves. Objectivity is a poison when there's suffering. We mustn't be silent. While your children are having a good time and enjoying life, hundreds of Jews aboard a ship near the South American coast have been refused permission to land by all the countries of that continent and are signing a declaration saying they will commit suicide if they are sent back to Germany. That's what we should be thinking about and nothing else.

Tell me, have you really considered what's going to happen to Grandmother and Grandfather? Have you really visualized their situation? If you ask me, something must be done. They can't possibly go on living as they are. How much longer shall we have them? Can't you really do anything for them? Or are you already working something out? If only I were in a position to help, I don't know what would be the most important thing for me to do. But in fact I'm not free. Couldn't we have a proper discussion about it? You mustn't think that what I'm saying is just hot air; concern for these poor prisoners haunts me night and day. We are now happy and outside while they, who have given us their love, must endure persecution alone. Is this right? Shouldn't we do everything to get them out? Isn't this our first and most pressing duty, quite apart from the love we feel for them? I think it is. I shall come back to this in my next letter.

Darling Mother, I wish you a happy stay in Varna.[16] And I kiss you with all my love.

Always your Peter

Faro, 14 July 1939

Dear Tina,

I was overjoyed to get your letter, although I haven't answered it before now. You told me so many things that I feel positively blank because nothing happens to me.

But first of all you must tell me how your first party went. Were you the queen of the ball? Did you dance a lot? How many admirers did you have? Did anyone particularly take your fancy? Are you in love, Tina, let me know at once. That seems to me a very urgent matter. I never thought that Fritz R. was exactly what you needed. You ought to love a fair young man who brings you flowers and is always terribly embarrassed when he speaks to you. And you'll find his embarrassment very amusing. And you'll know well how to hide your own embarrassment (because it's so new). That's how it should go. Perhaps you've found a young Bulgarian. It's such fun not to speak the same language and not to understand each other. And Slav blood has its charms—I myself was captivated by it as you know. But perhaps you prefer Northerners, who are our kith and kin.

Now I long for a photograph of you, especially as Mother told me that you're very pretty. You see I'm getting jealous, for I would happily take you out myself.

[16]His mother was preparing to spend several weeks at Saint-Constantine, near Varna, on the Black Sea, together with her two daughters and the "Old Man" who was bringing them to her.

Would you like that? Making a real night of it, till dawn? It would be such fun. To be absolutely honest, I can't yet quite imagine you as a young woman. In many respects you were still a baby when I left.

Which was quite a long time ago, wasn't it, when you come to think about it. I've already been in my funny little house here for ten and a half months. You must come with Mother and Angeli. That really would be something, don't you think so?

My dear Tina, the other side (of the page, of course) is for Angeli, which is why I'm finishing now. Write to me again and next time I write you I'll tell you about myself and Portugal. A loving kiss from your Peter.

Angelika, it's your turn now. Thank you for your letter. Write more from the left to the right and from the top to the bottom so that it's easier to read. But don't worry, I shall manage. How are you enjoying Varna? Take care of Mother. She has been waiting so long to have you with her!

It's marvellous that everything was so good for you in Berlin. Have you grown, like Tina, and will you soon be a lady? It's easier really to do it all in one go and stop being a child. I absolutely agree with you; grown-ups are so tiresome when they give themselves grown-up airs while they're often more childish than children could ever be. Confident that you understand me entirely, I kiss you.

Your Peter

Faro, 3 August 1939

Darling Mother,

All you women are obviously the same. When one wants precise information, one wants in vain. Thanks for the photographs. I always carry with me the one of Florinka the donkey with a ravishing sweet young Mother on her back. I'm never without it. God, what delight it gives me! Of course the Berthoffs, to whom I had to show it, couldn't possibly believe that . . . yes, yes, the same old story. I was as proud of you as of a sweetheart. Uncle Schr looks a bit battered and ready to say yes to everything, but it's nice to see him again. Angeli hasn't changed a bit—as sweet and cheeky and fair as ever. Give her a kiss (even two) from me and thank her for her long post-script.

I'm so glad you're feeling well at Saint-Constantine. You must all make the most of being there and build up your strength. You yourself must store it up for Sofia and the months to come. Just accumulate, and don't think about anything. And as for the primitive conditions, you really mustn't fuss about that; on this I'm in full agreement with Angeli. Is it really important? Where would I be if I'd always looked on these things with as critical an eye as you? We just shut our eyes and say good, good, and think no more about it. I now have a deep understanding for Sergette who, with matchless aristocracy, always lived as if there were some deep and hidden meaning in dirt. The fact she could never be persuaded to wash her neck derived from her concept of the world.

I'd love to know what you talked about with Uncle Schr (NB, I received his letter, very very nice). What I mean is; what are your short-term and middle-term plans? Are you staying in Bulgaria? Are you keeping the children with you? I'm in the dark, as usual. And how about your trip to Portugal? You wanted to come in September "at the latest". Have you forgotten already? Please, please, don't play hide-and-seek again! You say you miss me. Can't you imagine how much I miss you? There would be nothing lovelier for me, now at this moment, than to see you all and kiss you all—you in particular—and to be with you all for a while. I make the wish to every shooting star. Just think, it's now eleven months since I left. Do you remember our goodbye? How often I've been tortured by that scene at the Berlin Zoo station. It was all so short and you were so sad and so brave and I was so horrid to you! During the two months before my departure I should have been with you night and day. Darling Mother, how I reproach myself on this score! I shall always remember your smile as you went up the steps, a smile sadder than any tears. I saw it and felt it, and then there was that hardly perceptible gesture of yours—how you turned back towards me with your hand, suddenly raised, violently raised, hanging like a bird in the sky. I had nothing but the memory of a very distant sign, a sign from the past. And I didn't rush towards you though I knew full well it was the only thing to do, that our last moments were slipping by, but, you see, that's how we are . . .

Peter

Faro, 17 September 1939

Dearest Mother,

Your letter arrived the day before yesterday. Should I tell you that it surprised me? No doubt it was stupid of me but I hoped it would be quite different. I thought that the event[17] would be reflected in every single phrase, would impregnate each word with its colossal magnitude. But not a bit of it. It was a letter

[17]The war.

like many others, and if I wasn't already aware of the situation it would tell me nothing.

You don't want to say anything, of course. And please don't feel yourself obliged to break the silence that you've adopted simply because I myself can't help writing to you. Quite the reverse. You have relieved me immensely—not only by your reaction—which is firm, courageous, not giving way to panic—but also by the sheer existence of this letter from Bulgaria which has dispelled the gloomiest forebodings.

I shall now tell you everything I did. On 1 September I sent a telegram to Saint-Constantine. I wanted to be in close touch with you just as soon as possible and I wanted you to know this. I also thought that letters might no longer get through. In spite of which I also wrote to you on that day. Then as I got no reply I sent you a second telegram, in French this time, asking you to answer the first. At the same time I wrote you a letter in French. All this for fear that letters and telegrams in German wouldn't get through. As I still received no reply I thought you must have returned to Germany with the children shortly before the war started. I became practically certain of this when the post office informed me that the two telegrams could not be delivered because the addressee had left Saint-Constantine. Then the days passed until your letter came.

What I found so astonishing was that—quite apart from whether you received my letters and telegrams—you didn't yourself take the initiative of writing. Because my instinctive reaction was to get into touch with you at once. Perhaps you won't understand, perhaps you will simply note it as another example of the deep difference between our attitudes towards extraordinary events—you being strong, steady and silent, me exploding all over the place—but, believe me, my first impulse was to tell you and to tell just you: It's war and we're alive; it's war and we've got to realise it; it's war and we're in it.

Right, Mother, let's not talk about it any more. In any case I have nothing more to say although ideas are seething inside me. But they aren't ripe yet and could only worry you pointlessly.

I shall stop now and wait for your letters. Write as often as you can, I beg of you! And I shall do the same. I want to be told everything. And keep strong like you are today.

Have you any news of my grandparents, Mother?

We must take them into our innermost being and give proof of piety, in our fashion.

Goodbye. All my thoughts and all my love.

Your Peter

Faro, 15 October 1939

Dearest Mother,

I'm so delighted that all is going as you hoped and that you've got the children with you. Keep your eyes open and let me know at once if any change occurs where you are.

I was immensely happy to hear that my grandparents are safe and sound and well. You know how much I always worry about them. If only I could hear news of them direct!

I'm also delighted with the information you give me about Erich. We must show him our gratitude and try to protect him with our prayers. There has been a pause now, but don't let's have any illusions; what has happened is only a beginning. Its cruelty and horror ought to suffice for quite a while, but we must get used to the idea that we are living in a time of unparalleled excesses.

I went to Lisbon—for a few days I thought, but stayed for three weeks! It wasn't in vain because my position has now been clarified; I have been given my *carte d'identité*, valid for five years. That means I can now enjoy relative security and not live in constant fear of being expelled. I can now tell you that things have been very difficult for me for months and I had more or less prepared myself for a sudden departure and emigration elsewhere. I had hatched a lot of vague plans, all with very slender chances of success, written to ten consulates for information and envisaged various possibilities. Right, so all that now belongs to the past. Tomorrow I shall get back to work. Winter is coming and it's not really all that fun in my little house. Yet I'm glad to be back again. This calm and this vast sky and hardly anyone around!

Tina's adventure sounds very amusing. And the "tempo" doesn't suit her at all. What does she really say about it? Does she love the boy? I think that question can be asked again. She must tell me the whole story down to the last detail. I shall answer and you can rest assured that I shan't say anything silly. Obviously I wish her every possible good and that she won't be disappointed.

Write to me very soon, dearest Mother. Perhaps you don't realise how much you have changed. In every line of your letters I see you as strong, calm and well. That's what matters and what I longed for so much. I don't think I need be frightened any more. So carry on!

Kiss Angelika and Tina, pay my respects to the unknown one, I mean their Macedonian nobleman, and let yourself be hugged a thousand times by

Your Peter

Faro, 7 November 1939

Dearest Mother,

So I didn't see my good, dear Grandfather again after all! I always hoped and always thought I'd somehow get there in time. And now he's dead, so alone, so terribly alone! I can't tell you how agonisingly deeply I feel it. You say in your letter that I mustn't be sad, because all is well with him. But I don't believe all was well with him when he died, I think on the contrary that he cried a great deal inwardly at dying so alone and abandoned. Because there was only Grandmother with him. None of the others he had loved and lived his life for. Just imagine what it means, to have to die without one's children. What wouldn't he have given to have us all around him again, just to see us again, to say a word to us! No, Mother, I think he died a very unhappy death although he isn't suffering any more now. For if we had all been there, don't you see, it would have been quite a different death, an unclouded death as it were, a right death, a death that could be assimilated, because it's ineluctable, forms part of life and is taken for granted from the beginning. Not, as now, a haphazard death, a death without rhyme or reason which brings scandal wherever it strikes and leaves nothing but an ominous void. And how can we ourselves face death calmly, now that we know nothing about it? No, no, it wasn't a beautiful death and it certainly wasn't the death he should have had after such a life. I can't say any more except quote the lines that are constantly in my mind—by, forgive me, Rilke:

> O Lord, grant to each man the death that befits him,
> The death that flows from each life,
> Where he found love, significance and need.

And now, how about Grandmother? What is she doing? Who is with her? Is there someone always with her? Mother, you must promise me to do everything you can to see her. Don't say it wouldn't be wise just now and there are difficulties. That would be deplorable. There are difficulties everywhere but they can be overcome. If it is in any way possible, if it isn't absolutely impossible, then you really should go. If only for a day. It's not a matter of Grandfather any more, but of Grandmother, who, as you point out, is totally alone and without protection. If I could, I myself would go this very day, do believe me. And afterwards, indeed very soon, we must have her with us. She must live with you, and if that can't be managed, she must come to me. This idea may seem preposterous to you at first glance, but why not? I've enough money to have her here. We could take a little flat in town, and she wouldn't be alone because there are the Berthoffs' parents who have no one of their own age to talk to. And I would look after her and do anything on earth for her. And I'm sure she would feel well, and above all she wouldn't be lonely. And you would come later, perhaps for a visit, perhaps for good, and when finally Grandmother ceased to live, it would happen very differently from how it has this time.

But if you had her with you, which would be preferable from many points of view, I could send you a sum of money every month to help you out a little, starting at Christmas. It wouldn't be much—you know what I earn here—and in Germany it wouldn't go far, but if, as I suppose, the standard of life in Bulgaria is approximately the same compared with Germany as it is in Portugal, then it would be a sum worth having. I could send three hundred escudos every month, which is roughly equivalent to eleven hundred leva. Is that very little?

I want to tell you something, Mother, and you may find it strange, affected, sentimental and goodness knows what else. And yet I'm going to tell you regardless . . . This death has enabled me to see very clearly a truth that I've intuited for some time, namely the profound significance of custom. You see, in the olden days the dying blessed their children. The children came and knelt down and the old man laid his hand on each head. It was a fine and solemn gesture without which one didn't die and both parties desired it. And I find that I myself have this desire, or rather I did have it, and it makes me sad to see it unfulfilled. Not the ceremony itself, that's only symbolic and no one is free enough today to dare actually to bend the knee. But the hand perhaps, the great assent, and the transmission, and also the forgiveness. This being face-to-face and the linking of a life that is finished with a life that is yet to be lived, under the sign of goodness and compassion, in the full consciousness of giving and receiving. Grandfather was a simple man, you see, and his notions and principles were simple. There were many things he didn't understand, and he repudiated them because he didn't understand them. But his heart—what you call "his great heart full of love and goodness"—was rich, inexhaustibly rich. He understood everything with his heart. Few could match him in human richness and plenitude. Never, in the course of a long and often difficult life was he found wanting in goodness or humanity; he was always ready to sacrifice himself for others, and he spent himself in doing so. That in itself makes a human being great, that in itself is worthy of remembrance. Which is why, Mother, the hand, the blessing . . . I think that this contact would have meant a great deal to me, and perhaps to him too, as a symbol of my veneration and my love, both much greater than I've ever been able to show or express. For our powers of expression are very feeble, and it is so difficult for our inner being to reveal itself to the outside when we find ourselves face to face! There are always obstacles, due to our habits of life, obstacles men in the past weren't aware of because gestures and expressions were much more spontaneous then than they are with us now. And this is why we need symbols, gestures that bring us together and express what we personally suppress but nevertheless feel. Yes, I think a final and solemn goodbye of this kind would have been important, in the context of things that have happened and things that are to come. Our sole hope now is that Grandmother can hold out and that she may somehow contrive to join us. It's my dearest hope. And please write to me as soon as you can about anything you may have gleaned about Grandfather. On what day he died, for instance. I've only got one small photograph of him, the one taken in the garden at Wannsee, and it's now terribly blurred. And I must say this to end up with: We weren't very good children to him, neither you nor I. We should have been much more concerned with the grandparents, and even at that it would have been but a pale shadow of the love they both gave to us. But we thought we had more important things to do and in fact all we did was "to visit them now and again." And that is why—as I now realise—I never properly said goodbye to them when I left.

I appreciate that you must be having problems with the children and this worries me a lot. I don't want to seem boring, but I do implore you to let me know exactly what your situation is. And I hope with all my heart that you'll make out for the best, my darling. And the same goes for Erich—if you can write to him, do give him my love. I can easily believe you when you say you would like to have him again. Perhaps that will happen. Everything is far too provisional for us to be certain even of the worst. And resignation is not the most logical conclusion to draw from our lives. Everything is possible and this is why we should go on saying to each other, hope, courage, patience.

I shall end now, and you will know from this letter what to say to Grandmother from me should you visit her.

Goodbye my darling, and kiss the kids a thousand times for me. Write soon. All my love, and I kiss you.

Always your Peter

If there's anything at all I can give you, just tell me. Do you need money? Goodbye, I love you.

Lisbon, 1 December 1939

Dearest Mother,

I'm writing to you from Lisbon where I've been for several days putting certain affairs in order. You must certainly know from your Bulgarian experiences that worries nowadays never end, even when one thinks one's settled everything. My worries are small but time-consuming and require endless procedures. Good, that's the end of that, it isn't very serious. I found Grandmother's letter very moving. Poor little woman, what's going to become of her? The proposal I made in my last letter—to have her here—has turned out to be impracticable, alas: the only difficulties, but they're pretty big, are those of immigration and at the moment they appear to be insurmountable. People are extremely strict and intolerant, as you yourself know from experience. All countries are the same in this respect. So what can we do? We must hope, and organize things for the future. Not too easy when we don't know what the future holds and whether Grandmother can hold out as long as that!

You're in a sorry plight again, Mother darling, so alone and abandoned. I'd like to think that Tina will come back.[18] But in no case must you relapse into the despondency of your first days in Sofia, which you have overcome. With a little goodwill you will resist it. And then you really must remember how fortunate you are compared with people who have nothing but anguish to look forward to. Think of the Jews in Lublin, think of the men at the front, think of the thousands of victims of an almost generalized violence. What do our worries matter compared with that? Can we even speak of *our* worries?

Grandmother's letter gives a blow by blow account of Grandfather's death and now I know that it was quick and kind. It's good to have this assurance though it doesn't in any way diminish the sorrow. But how I would love to have seen him again!

Tell me about Angeli—is she still with you? It seems incredible that such difficulties could be made about a child of eleven. With Tina it's more understandable, but with the little one . . .

You have the great advantage over me of being able to listen to music. I miss it so much. In January Weingartner is coming here and generally speaking there are now all sorts of concerts I would love to follow. But how? I can't come in to Lisbon specially, and when I'm here there's nothing.

This is already becoming a long letter, dearest

[18]Bettina, the elder daughter, had to return to Berlin in November, 1939, because the German embassy in Sofia refused to extend the validity of her passport. She managed to get back to Bulgaria at the end of January. The mother feared that she would also have to be separated from the younger one, Angelika. But this came to nothing.

Mother, and please answer it as soon as possible. Tell me all about yourself, who you're meeting, if you have any friends, in short give me a picture of all that concerns you. Again we're somehow drifting apart from each other, and that mustn't happen. Goodbye, my darling, and remember that I have a huge longing to see you. I kiss you a thousand times and give you all my love.

Your Peter

19 December 1939

Dear little Angelika,

For your birthday, for Christmas and the New Year—for all these events rolled into one I wish you the best and loveliest thing that I can imagine. My very special wish is that you may be able to stay on with our mother so as to help her through this difficult period, and that you will enjoy doing so.

But if my wish isn't granted you mustn't be sad. We're all of us going through black periods, you know, and we must face them as cheerfully as possible. Because times will change. For instance—and you can think about it already—the time will come when we shall all be reunited and then our happiness will be so tremendous that these bad days will count for nothing. So accept all the love I give you and help, help people whenever you have the chance! And do you know the way to do that? You do it by not thinking about yourself and your miseries because that does no good at all.

A thousand kisses from your brother.

Peter

2 March 1940

Dearest Mother,

Many thanks for your welcome birthday letter and the delightful photograph of Tina. God, how pretty she is! I simply hadn't realised how pretty she was. And she has exactly your eyes! Kiss her for me.

I can't write at length today because I have so much to do. Don't be cross, I'll soon write in greater detail. But I want to give you news as soon as possible because you're always worried if you don't hear, for however short a while. But in fact you've not the slightest reason to worry, and if I fall ill—as you seem to fear—I do assure you there are lots of people here ready to look after me and make a fuss over me. So you must try to realise that it's the same as if I were at home, and be absolutely calm.

You're surely a little happier now as you've got both the girls with you. But has Tina's position now been clarified? Can she stay permanently or will all the tiresome business start again? And how is Angeli? Is she better? The mountains and the snow will do her good, will do you all good. So just rest and take advantage of them!

It's winter here too, and appallingly cold as it is everywhere else. And without a stove it's no joke. But the experience of last winter helps me as it does you; I dream about the sun and heat and would like to be on the equator.

But seriously, what's your opinion of this winter? It's not been as cold as this for decades, apparently. It's as if some superior force were trying to bog down the war. A nice thought, but, alas, a futile one. We all know that when the thaw comes . . . but better not think about it!

For you, all my love and a huge nostalgic longing from

Your Peter

In November, 1939, Salazar, following Hitler's orders, had decided to rid Portugal of all German Jews. When Peter Schwiefert wrote this last letter he had already been arrested and imprisoned for over three months. He had told his mother nothing about it (see the letter of 19 December 1939 which gives no address) so as to spare her anxiety, and it was only after his release and expulsion that he wrote to her from Rome to tell her what had happened, though even then he made as little as possible of what he had been through. He was unaware that she had been kept informed of events by a friendly couple with whom she was in correspondence and that in fact he had been released solely through her efforts and her money.

Rome, 13 March 1940

My dearest Mother,

I haven't written until today because it wouldn't have made any sense to have written before. I left Portugal on the 8th—I don't know whether you know this or not. I stayed for three days in Barcelona and arrived here in Rome this very afternoon by plane. On Sunday I push on to Brindisi and thence to Athens where I shall settle. I've got a visa for several months and hope to be able to regularize my position for longer.

Concerning what happened in Portugal, I don't want to tell you everything in detail just now because it would take too long. I must get off this letter quickly so that you have news of me, and in any case the whole story is not the most important thing at the moment. In a word, they refused to extend my visa and I was forced to get out, like many other foreigners. The Jewish Committee paid my fares. A friend of mine, herself a member of the Committee, gave me a little money to tide me over my first days in Athens. She has helped me a great deal. Please realise that I'm not to blame if you've been anxious. I kept silent on purpose so that you wouldn't be pointlessly worried about me. Because I know you so well! Why should I torture you with my problems? You see I couldn't possibly have known that you would receive that idiotic message from the Wieners. That's why I say I wasn't to blame. But, blame or no, there's no reason for depression. I'm in good health and am again venturing forth, even if I don't exactly want to. I shall arrive fit and well in Athens and shall work and live there very much as I did in Portugal. And the gorgeous dream I've been cherishing for so long will at last come true; we shall see each other. This makes me so happy. Because you'll be able to come to Athens, won't you . . . It isn't far.

I have been delayed writing this letter for the following reasons: it was only three days before my departure that I was informed of your application to the Lisbon Committee, and during those three days I didn't have a moment to write, quite apart from the fact that I hoped to have a communication direct from you before writing myself. Your letter arrived at the last moment. It was handed to someone who wasn't able to make comtact with me and I left Lisbon without it.

I then intended to write to you during my journey through Spain, but realised that the local censorship would cause yet another week's delay. So that's why I've waited until now.

And now what other things will you have been imagining, my dearest one? Such absurdities! You must understand that once I'm in Athens not only shall I be able to start giving lessons immediately but I've also got the job of representing my former firm, through which I hope to earn a lot of money. And life in Greece is ten times cheaper than in Portugal.

I had to come by plane, because with my German passport I would have been captured by the Allies had I come by boat. But that danger is now over and I shall make my way slowly towards Hellas. The flight was in fact as boring as the train journey from Lisbon to Madrid and Barcelona was exhausting. Half a day and a night to Madrid, and the following night another fourteen hours to Barcelona. And all in third class. I don't really know how I managed to keep upright. I stayed three days in Barcelona (Spain is a country one can't describe, ghastly!) and while there met up with a friend and his fiancée who had left a week before me and for the same reason. But the Committee had paid their fares only as far as Barcelona. No further. So there they still are — without money, without work, desperately waiting for their tickets to Athens (at first we had hoped to travel together). I never stop writing to Lisbon to ask that something be done for them. I hope things will work out, because the life of both of them is literally at stake. At first I meant to wait for them here, but it's impossible, so I'm going on ahead. Once in Greece, we intend to work together. We'll have to see. And now, my darling, I think I've reassured you — if you were anxious about your dear son. Everything else can be said by word of mouth, very soon I hope. And once I set about telling the whole story, where on earth will I begin!

And one more thing please—if the Wieners have told you endless tales about me needing help and things going badly for me, don't take any notice. I don't need anything and it's pointless for you to try to raise money. Everything is going for the best.

I kiss you a thousand times and let me say again what unbounded joy I feel at the thought of seeing you again. And tell the children how much I love them.

Goodbye, dear Mother, and see you soon! I kiss you.

Your Peter

Traveling by plane I was only able to bring one suitcase. All my luggage is still in Lisbon. The woman I told you about was planning to send it to Athens by boat. But if this doesn't work out (because it might be seized!) can she send it to you? You wouldn't have to do anything except take it in and then keep it. Everything would have been paid in Lisbon. But I'll write about this again.

Athens, 28 March 1940

Darling Mother,

I arrived in Athens this morning where your letter was awaiting me. The journey from Lisbon has taken three weeks all told. As there is a mass of things to explain and discuss I shall begin by going straight to the essentials if you don't mind. The rest can come later. I shall start by answering your questions point by point.

My journey—absolutely no point in further elaboration, because you know how it was. I myself don't know how I got through it but I'm prepared to believe that I have a guardian angel who always steps in at the crucial moment. Without the angel, everything would be unbelievable from beginning to end. Suffice it to say that I am now in Athens and that a new chapter is beginning.

My letter from Rome—it soft-pedalled everything on purpose; I was sounding the ground to find out what you knew and what you didn't. I didn't realise that you knew all. My intention, as during the previous few months, was to spare you pointless anxiety by saying only what was strictly necessary and by presenting my position as tolerable. I can now admit that it wasn't. That fourteen-week period in Lisbon was very tough and I really did go through the mill. I couldn't have endured it much longer. But more about that later. That you knew about my arrest as long ago as the beginning of February is one of the great surprises of your letter. Why didn't you tell me so at once? I can't remember very well your letters of that period, but one thing I'm absolutely convinced of, that you never made the faintest allusion to it. Now that you admit how worried you were I see how entirely justified my silence was. As I took it for granted that you couldn't do anything to help me, and as I hoped up to the last minute that I would extricate myself thanks to the Jewish Committee, it seemed utterly pointless to worry you for nothing.

The second surprise of your letter is that you wrote to the Committee and to the Wieners. I had no idea that you had moved into action. The Committee told me absolutely nothing about it. Neither about your efforts nor about your financial assistance. I assumed—until today—that the Committee, and the Committee alone, had paid my fares. The only sign from you was passed on to me by Madame Mathilde Beusaude (the woman I told you about); she told me you had written to the

Committee asking for news of me. And I implored Madame Beusaude not to tell you anything about me as I wanted to do that myself.

And I knew nothing, either, about the money you sent. It is true that without it I wouldn't have been allowed to leave Portugal (I was in prison right up to the moment that I took my place in the train). But that you had to sacrifice your allowance for several months so as to help me hits me very hard. I knew nothing about it and did all I could so that you wouldn't have to take on such a burden. I wanted to avoid the very thing that happened. Now that it's done and that I realise I would never have got out without your help, and that I would still be in prison, please accept all my thanks. You literally saved me.

As for Greece, I didn't choose this country. But Greece presented me with the only way of getting out once the Brazil solution had fallen through. I had put in a request for Brazil a long time before and at first I thought it would work. But the visa was refused and for the following reason: The policeman who accompanied me to the Consulate was known there and hence they knew that I had been arrested. It was only the Greek consul who was still prepared to allow me into his country and this for the sole reason that I already had a Yugoslav visa in my pocket. All other possibilities were excluded.

America — I've been enrolled on their quota and perhaps I shall get there in a few years provided I obtain a good *affidavit*. I didn't want Spain or Italy for obvious reasons. South and Central America are out of the question if one hasn't got money or relations in those countries (the minimum demanded everywhere is a guarantee of 500 dollars). As for Brazil, I was dying to go there but there are two insurmountable obstacles. First, transport—as a German with a passport that does not bear the letter "J", I wouldn't get through the English control point. Secondly, there's the refusal of a visa by the Consulate in Lisbon. So only the Balkans remained. I could go to Yugoslavia—and also surely to you, for I imagine a Bulgarian visa would be easy to get there. That I shall see about, but not just yet. In one way or another a means will be found. When you say that I'm acting irresponsibly and without sufficient thought you're talking absolute nonsense. If I were, my situation would be better. But it is not the case and you ought to realise that I can't do anything else at the moment but try Greece.

I have no choice, and that's all there is to it. One thing is certain: It's terribly difficult and I don't know what's going to happen. I'm in a situation where I must always expect the worst, and that's what I'm doing. I have no solid support left. My most demanding adventure has now started, with my expulsion from Portugal. The vital thing is that I should settle down somewhere, but how, that's what I don't know at the moment. So please understand, Mother—just as soon as I settle down and start work, then I shall get straight, then I shall be saved. But I'm not there yet. For the moment I've got to keep up my spirits in the face of ill-luck and take what I'm offered, whatever it may be. If I can't stay here, I shall have to go elsewhere, and if that doesn't work out, then elsewhere again, and so on until a miracle perhaps happens or the war ends. What more can I say? I shall try to do my best. You say that people should avoid getting into a mess. Very pretty, but I'm there, I'm in a mess, and not through my fault. I was driven for no reason out of a country where I'd lived modestly and peaceably for a year and a half. I've landed up in a void (or in a mess, if you prefer) and now I must see whether there's anything I can hitch onto (a little star, perhaps!). I'm not in a position to pick and choose, so there's no question of "acting irresponsibly and without sufficient thought" (forget about my letter from Rome), on the contrary it's extremely serious, and I know it, and the only thing I can say to soothe you is to assure you that I'm adaptable and by and large not easily beaten. I've a considerable capacity for endurance in adversity and what's more I now have very few demands. I've learned to be satisfied with little. If I add that I seem always able to find people prepared to help me, then really there's no reason to give up hope. I must stick it out, I will stick it out, I won't give in. That's absolutely certain!

My one goal is to leave Europe. I never lose sight of it, I'm thinking about it all the time.

Your Peter

Athens, 29 March 1940

My darling,

Your second letter has just arrived. I've slept a little and feel better. The last part of the journey was appalling. I didn't shut my eyes for three nights in succession. Yesterday my legs were like rubber. I walked about the streets of Athens smiling like an imbecile and with my eyelids always closing.

So . . . thank you a thousand times for all the love contained in your letter. If only you knew, my sweet, how much I love you and how immense is my longing to see you . . . Oh please do come soon, it isn't far. How much does it cost? Can you raise a little money to get here? Personally I've none, none at all!

And now at last I'm going to tell you the truth: I arrived here without a penny. As I had to make a roundabout journey involving long delays in Barcelona, Rome, and Brindisi, all the money I brought with me from Lisbon simply went with the wind. The final part of my journey was paid for by the Greek agent at Brindisi and a chap I met in a car in northern Greece. I'll tell you the sequel later—the intervention of my guardian angel! Anyway, as soon as I arrived I went to the Committee. Though no letter of introduction had yet arrived there from the Lisbon Committee (though they had promised me they would send one and I'd written to them from Rome most urgently about it), the Committee here decided to help me—though it's not easy for them as I'm only a half-Jew, of non-Jewish confession, and I've a German passport without the "J" —which makes the outcome difficult to assess. Nevertheless they gave me a little money and sent me to a hotel paid for by the Committee. I've a clean decent room which I share with one other person. I'm saving the money for food and vital expenses. They're going to go on helping me, they tell me, but I'm not going to be allowed to work. For that I need a work permit and I won't be able to get one. Well, I'll see. If I give lessons no one need know. This evening I'm going to have a talk with a Greek recommended by my friend Morgan, the one who's still in Barcelona. I'll ask him not only about lessons but about the business of representing my Portuguese firm. He'll be able to tell me what's what. I'm not at all down-hearted.

My main problem is the police who'll soon be wanting to summon me. I've a three-months' visa and I hope to be left in peace for at least that amount of time. The residence permit has to be renewed every month. Perhaps they're being cautious because I haven't any money. If they want a guarantee I shall make use of the first valuable thing I receive—a parcel or something—and I shall show it to them.

To all my questions the Committee replied that they did not yet know what decision would be taken in my regard. Could I stay here, I asked, would I have to leave? At the worst there is—as a first stage—the Yugoslav solution. So now I need precise details concerning Bulgaria: Is it possible to get in? How can I obtain a residence permit or a work permit? Can I, failing the latter, give lessons and do translations? Or represent my sardine firm? Please answer all these questions carefully. Were I to arrive with a tourist visa, would it be very difficult for me to stay on? Is there a Jewish Committee there?

If there is, make contact with it. Find out about everything. Then write to me at once. If things go really badly here, if I have to decamp, and if circumstances seem a little more favourable in Bulgaria, then obviously I ought to try it out. Couldn't you and I set up shop together? Go into business in a small way? A restaurant, for instance? Could you find a backer? As for me, I'd do anything at all. I speak several languages: English, German, Portuguese and—tolerably (some people think perfectly)—French. How about your project of a beauty parlour? You would deal with the clients and I with the accounts. And how about a restaurant, prettily arranged, with culinary specialities, perhaps music? Of a type that doesn't exist—or hardly—in Sofia. Got up with taste—make contact with various poor artists—properly decorated, a pianist, so indispensable for thinking. In short, something original (horrid word, but you know what I mean) along the lines of Mikosh, in Berlin! It shouldn't be very difficult once someone put up the money. Or perhaps something diametrically opposed. A very, very cheap café, without tables, just the counter. Not like Quick—we would serve a proper meal. Soup, and then a simple dish but so cheap that even people with no money would go away satisfied. I've seen that in Rome—a Tavola Calda. It's full to bursting from morning till night, and you make money. And virtually no equipment, so not much initial outlay, just a small amount of capital would suffice. Think about it. God, I'm sure it would work with a little spunk. I'd buy a dress suit and do the honours (only in the first situation, of course!). The important thing is to get cracking—I'm learning Bulgarian already. Or a bar—it's all the same. Perhaps you yourself have an idea; as for me, I shall go on searching. All we're missing is a money man, but you can find one can't you? So write to me at once and in detail about Sofia.

And don't worry, my darling, I'm being helped in these early stages. I'll pull through as always. But you're being unfair when you suggest that I was in any way responsible for my arrest and expulsion. You can't think what dirty tricks go on in Portugal. It's a country full of bandits and loathsome cops. Yes. I'll tell you all about it some time. But anyway, I'm absolutely innocent. No one can reproach me with anything!

Don't try to send me parcels. I'm all right for the moment, with the Committee's help. Subsistence is not the problem at the moment. It's the future that's the problem. For the time being all is well, you mustn't worry. I've got food and lodging. My passport is still the old one, without the "J". Otherwise I wouldn't have even got the Greek visa.

Come as soon as you can. It's vital that we should discuss everything together and examine all the possibilities now that we are so close to each other. So come, that's what matters, quite apart from my desire to see you. Or should I be the one to come? If so I'm sure the Committee will lend me the fare. But write!

Rio would be the best solution, as I've said before. Palestine—only as a last resort, if everything else fails.

But write to Bruno[19] all the same, or to the Hirsches—one never knows.

And now I shall finish. This letter has become a positive discourse.

Goodbye, my darling. Kiss the children for me. With all tenderness and love,

Your Peter

Athens, 5 April 1940

Darling Mother,

See what happens when I write to you frankly! It's always the same; you go "meschugge"[20] with fear! But it was stupid to try to give a valid account in a first letter and on a first impression. Nothing is so bad as I had thought; everything becomes clearer with the passage of time.

To come down to facts: Things are going much better on all fronts. In the week since I've been here I've followed every imaginable trail, scent, hint, suggestion, and I've already had some results. I've four irons in the fire, that is to say people are busying themselves on my behalf in four different directions. I've got to know quite a few people and they're all prepared to help me. They're doing the impossible and it will work. So listen: To start off with, there are two emigrants here, artists, who are making out marvellously and have the most fantastic contacts. They're looking around for a firm that will employ me. If they find one, the firm will put in a request for a work

[19]See p. 154.
[20]Yiddish word for "mad"

permit, and once this has been granted I shall easily obtain a residence permit. (As to residence, this is how things go: I can stay a month, that is until the 26th, without going to the police. And I'm told there won't be any problem for the following month either; it's only later that the difficulties will start.) If these two men's efforts come to nothing, they know a woman who's an intimate friend of the most important person in this country (you know who). If she agrees to step in, a single conversation will suffice and all will be settled.

My second protector is a dealer who is very in with the Portuguese Consulate, and he is helping me on two fronts. First — my sardine business. He sells to local wholesalers and if he sells I get a commission. This is how it happens: I receive supplies from Portugal and then transmit them to the dealer in question who in his turn gets into contact with the wholesalers. Today I'm writing to Cabecadas who in any case promised me his support. So if the sales take place the ice is broken and it will continue. And I shall receive my share.

Moreover my dealer said, "Don't worry about your residence permit. Let me have your passport shortly before the expiration date and I'll fix everything. You'll certainly be able to stay."

Then there's also someone who's looking for import-export companies in the Piraeus on my behalf. And finally there's a Greek couple that's trying to place me in rich families as private tutor, language teacher, chauffeur, or whatever. So you see all that's being done for me, dear Mother. Surely at least one of these initiatives will come to something? That's why I'm optimistic again, as I say, and I'm only sorry I sent you that letter which caused you unnecessary anxiety. If you consider that four parallel moves are being made on my behalf and that hope is being held out to me on four fronts, then surely you realise there's no need to worry_ about me. I shall pull through as I always have done. It's the pure truth—I'm not saying all this just to reassure you. I promised I would stop concealing things from you.

So you're terribly frightened at the thought of me turning up in Bulgaria without warning. Don't worry, I shan't come. I just wanted to know what things are like there because it's good to examine all the possibilities. I perfectly understand your reasons; but now, Mother, I expect your immediate arrival in Athens. You must come at once!

At last the Lisbon Committee has telegraphed the Greek Committee to tell them that everything I said is true and that they must help me. They will therefore continue to do so, but they are the only people who can't help in obtaining my residence permit because, as I'm only "fifty percent", they haven't the right to enroll me on their registers (which deal only with the "hundred percents") and hence to represent me before the police. They say, "Try to work things out for yourself, you've got plenty of contacts now. There's nothing we can do, however much we want to. As for short-term help, we'll give it to you until you're in a position to sort things out for yourself."

So that briefly is the balance sheet of this last week: plenty of people ready to stand by me and give me their support. The general opinion is that it will be hard to solve all my problems, even very hard, but that there's no need for despair. At least one of these enterprises ought to succeed, and indeed will succeed.

And now I say again: Come, so that we can discuss everything more fully. Come as soon as you can, if possible before 25 April. Come at once—what keeps you in Sofia? The children can manage very well without you for a day or two. Or why not bring them, if your money can stretch that far? But the really important thing is that you and I should meet at the first possible moment.

If you could get some positive decision concerning Bolivia it would be wonderful. Please, please get busy. I would leave at once if only I had the means. Above all we mustn't make the mistake of those emigrants who let America slip through their fingers because things seemed to be going well in the countries where they found first refuge. I agree with you entirely; Greece is only a stepping stone. However, I have to behave as if I wanted to stay—because one never knows . . .

And is Brazil absolutely out of the question? Because it would be even better than Bolivia.

Naturally I won't say no to your offer of a small allowance, because I can only just manage with what I've got. But I hope that the sardine business will work out and that some money will come in from that. Everything will be all right. Just a little patience, that's all. If the enterprise gets on its feet I shall perhaps be able to open an office of my own. Free premises have already been put at my disposal. So you see all that's being done for me.

And let me say again: Please don't worry about me turning up in Bulgaria. To begin with, I wouldn't do anything before discussing it with you, and then if the situation really is as you describe it I'm considerably better off here. And you must stop worrying about me. I'm well, I eat well, I sleep well, and have in a general way absolutely recovered. There's no question of my being "looked after" because I'm in perfect health, a little thin perhaps, but that's understandable. And I've got the strength to pull through here, whether it be to stay on or to set off elsewhere.

So I shall in no circumstances descend on you or

bring you "misfortune", my dearest Mother, but I'll wait for you here in Athens, where everyone is charming. I kiss you a thousand times.

Your Peter

There's absolutely no problem before the 25th. And by then I shall have taken a big step forward.

Athens, 11 April 1940

My darling,

I'm waiting for your letter. All mail should be addressed to the *poste restante* because I'm moving in a day or two and don't yet know where I shall be. Listen, it's very, very important: You absolutely must be here before the 24th or 25th of April. On that date my permitted time expires and it is vital that I should have talked to you before then. None of the steps taken on my behalf have yet given results, and though people try to outdo each other in saying that things are following a normal course, these things are still so doubtful that nothing definite can be envisaged. So come at once, and let me know by telegram or express letter the day of your arrival. I must talk to you before the 25th.

My longing to see you is indescribable and I kiss you.

Peter

Can you please tell me when the money will arrive? When did you send it?

Athens, 20 April 1940

My darling,

Just got your letter. I'm utterly overjoyed that you've decided to come so soon. You can't imagine how

I long for your arrival, my sweet love! Tuesday, then, the 23rd, at half past six, I'll be at the airport.

Tell me, why are you so frightened for me? It simply doesn't make sense. Even if none of the plans have yet borne fruit there's no need to lose hope (knock on wood). You must stop taking such a black view of things, there'll always be a *modus vivendi*. But all further details by word of mouth!

On Tuesday you'll be here! I kiss you endlessly.

Your Peter

Athens, 24 April 1940

Tell me what's happened. This is the second evening I've waited for you and you haven't come! And no word from you, no letter, no telegram, nothing! Has something happened? Are you ill? Yet I wrote and told you that I'd meet you on Tuesday, that is yesterday, at seven o'clock. Didn't you get that letter? I'm utterly bewildered and terribly worried. Let me know at once why you didn't come. Are there difficulties? Write by express letter and tell me the exact time of your arrival. I shan't be at the airport myself but you'll receive instructions there from the flight manager.

Kisses, and *come!*

Peter

Athens, Thursday 25 April 1940

To recapitulate, Mother darling: I received your letter on Saturday the 20th announcing your (probable) arrival on Tuesday the 23rd at seven in the evening. I answered the same day—by air mail—to say I'd be waiting for you on Tuesday. Given that there are no flights on Saturday (which I didn't know) my letter wouldn't have reached you till Tuesday at the earliest. So I expected you on Tuesday and then again yesterday—but neither yesterday nor the day before was there any Mother, nor any news either. I then sent you a postcard, still, of course, by air mail. And today I get three letters from you: the first two this morning, one dated Monday (a day and a half late), the other Tuesday (a day late), and the third—your express letter of Wednesday—now this moment (half a day late). So you see how precarious our contact is. Each letter waits in the post office for an indeterminate period during which it's presumably being opened and censored.

So I shall start by answering the first of your three letters.

It wasn't possible for me to ring you on Monday or Tuesday. Today is Thursday and I hesitate to do so because I'm afraid I won't be able to get you at your home. I wanted to send you a telegram to tell you to phone me this evening but I abandoned the idea because it costs 150 drachmas. So please ring me at Athens 30651 on Friday evening between eight and eleven if this letter arrives on Friday afternoon; if not, ring me on Saturday at the same time.

Now your second letter. Obviously I'm disappointed. But it isn't too serious if you come at the beginning of May. If no other course is open then neither you nor I can do anything about it. You must cope with the problem of the five thousand leva as quickly as possible and then come (I suspected you had difficulties in that quarter).

I've been to the police and I'll know on the 30th whether my residence permit can be extended. It's unlikely that they'll refuse given it's the first time, and the first time it always works. I daren't say so for certain, but I think I can say that this first month is guaranteed.

I've booked a hotel room for you at 70 drachmas a day, with a ten per cent reduction if you stay more than ten days. It's impossible to find a suitable hotel or boarding house at a cheaper rate. Sixty drachmas for a single room is the minimum. Only rooms in a private house would be cheaper. But if the hotel price is too high then I'll tell you what we can do: You can take my room for the length of your stay and I'll go to a very cheap hotel. Secondly, if you come by plane, it's unlikely I'd be able to meet you at the airport because the company's coach is reserved for passengers and a taxi would be too expensive. And it's difficult to hire a private car. So if I can't come the coach will put you down at the Grand Bretagne Hotel in the centre of the town and I'll be waiting for you there.

I think that's everything. It would be marvellous if you managed to pull off Bolivia. But I must point out that I would need a *laissez-passer* from the English for that journey—they would make me leave the ship if I only had my German passport without the "J".

Spring has come to this country and it's warm at last! It must be unbearable in summer. I'm well, my only trouble being that I'm unable to work. I've tried everything, but nothing has resulted from my efforts and nothing will.

Your thousand leva have gone already—swallowed up by urgent clothes repairs, laundry, postal charges, repayment of debts, and so on. Everything is so expensive here, and when one wants to have a good meal just for once, then the Committee's whole monthly allowance goes on it. Yet God knows I'm not extravagant, you must believe me.

Enough for the moment. Kiss the children. I hug you with all my infinite love and my even greater longing to see you.

Your Peter

Please let me know the exact day, hour and place of your arrival. I couldn't bear to wait for you in vain again. It's terrible to be so full of joy and hope and all for nothing! The number 30651 where you should ring is the King George Hotel. I haven't got a telephone where I am.

Athens, 30 April 1940

It was so gorgeous to talk to you! Although your voice was so sad because of the disappointment. But what does it matter in the long run? A small delay, that's all, which means nothing after so many years of waiting. You'll come soon, in ten days or a fortnight, and then we'll have forgotten all about it. And besides we would have been very surprised, you and I, if everything had gone without a hitch the first time. Nothing goes smoothly nowadays. And thank you, Mother, for telephoning. And now you must come!

No news here. No decision has yet been made—that's for the day after tomorrow. But I've something else in view—I'll talk to you about it—and I'm a bit depressed because I'm beginning to have had enough of the city, not of Athens, no, but of the city, you understand! But what does it matter—the crucial thing is to see you, and quickly.

Peter

I love you.
Kiss the children. Tell them to write!

Athens, 3 May 1940

My darling,

Thank you for your last letter, but I think you're beginning to get a bit peculiar. For instance now you suddenly don't want to come because some of your friends have warned you against it! How you love taking other people's advice! Yet you're usually so independent. So no more words, my dear — this trip must be made, and as soon as possible! You must overcome all difficulties and obstacles—because I want to see you, and you want it too! Please, please don't put it off for another day. What your horoscope says is of total indifference to me and you can tell those people from me that they can mind their own business and not interfere with things they don't understand. For they couldn't possibly know how vital it is for us to see each other. And even if you made the trip solely because I wanted you to, it would still be amply justified. What the hell really matters at this moment? What have we got apart from our love? What's the point of living if we always have to do violence to our feelings? Don't you see that we must finish once and for all with all this chit-chat about what's prudent and what's wise and what's right and what isn't? That you should come is right and good and necessary because we both want it and need it in the deepest part of ourselves. That's the sole valid justification for anything! And that's all that need be said, because it's really too absurd to go into lengthy cogitation as to whether two people who haven't seen each other for years and are only a few hours' journey apart should meet or not.

You ask whether it wouldn't be preferable to send me the money you would otherwise have spent on the journey—a question it's utterly superfluous to answer. I have enough to live on, I can manage, and, as you already know, I've other things in view. So stop worrying about me—how many times must I repeat this? It's time wasted. Your sole preoccupation should be to *come.* Then you will see if I really resemble you, as you say . . . Why were the children "pale with emotion" during our telephone call? Were they with you? And if so, why didn't you let me have a word with them? I kiss them a thousand times and hold you in my arms with all my love and wild longing to see you. Come quickly!

Forgive me, but who does Erich think he is when he says I ought to go back? Is he just making idle chatter or does he still not realise what I think and who I am?

Your Peter

Athens, 7 May 1940

My darling,

I've had no news since your letter of 1 May. Why don't you write? What's happening? Please give me a sign of life immediately. I expect you on 15 May at the latest. If you don't come in the course of next week then it's no good. There's nothing to worry about, nothing has happened, everything's the same, but now a decision really must be made. For if you always go back on your word then I'm left hanging in the air and don't know what choice to make. Do you understand? So please stop dithering, do what's necessary, and come! I need to talk to you, immediately, it's getting absurd! And write, do you hear?

All my love and thousands of kisses.

Peter

Athens, 13 May 1940

Dearest Mother,

Many thanks for your letters of the 8th and 10th and I quite see that, alas, you can't get away at once. Yet—setting all emotions to the side—I still maintain it's absolutely vital that you and I should meet and talk as soon as possible. To explain everything in writing is out of the question—one has to be prudent. That's why I was wondering whether there wasn't some way of expediting things by proceeding along other lines, by sending you, for instance, an invitation accompanied by a declaration in due form. This might enable you to receive more easily the authorization to take out currency. I could obtain such an invitation pretty quickly. But I very much doubt if Erich would be able to come. Regulations concerning foreigners (and particularly, of course, Germans) are getting stricter every day, as you must know. Indeed I've heard from a reliable source that Germans can no longer come in. And you must also know that what has happened in the West could happen here at any moment.[21] After that all travelling would be at an end and we'd never see each other again. So I beseech you to do all you can and not lose another hour.

And now something else, something crucial: I've the possibility of obtaining a Brazilian visa without any great difficulty. A six-months' tourist visa, but that would suffice. Because once there one could get it extended. But where to find the fare? The price of the crossing to Rio is about two hundred dollars. They don't demand proof-of-support on arrival (of course you have to have a few pennies in your pocket, but no specified sum). So it would be very simple, if only

[21]The German offensive of 10 May in Western Europe.

there were more time before the departure date. Everything would have to be fixed up in less than two months, in other words I'd have to be ready to embark between the 15th and 30th of July at the latest to arrive in Brazil round about the 15th August. The dates are exactly the same with regard to Bolivia. The situation is that all journeys to South America have to be prepared within the next two months. After which I couldn't go (the reasons for this I can only explain by word of mouth). So you see how vital the time element is. Please realise that! By the way let me know at once what, if anything, you've been able to glean about Bolivia. I can't understand why you preserve such stony silence on this matter. I must know where I stand. The essential thing is the price of the fare. What solution have you in mind? Answer at once. As for my residence permit, nothing has changed. I presented myself at the police station on the specified date and was given a form with another date. So I presented myself again but only to be informed that my case hadn't yet come up and that I must wait for another summons. That was two weeks ago.

I was very surprised by something you said in one of your letters. You speak (exactly as you did in the past) of some kind of "duty" and some kind of "right" (concerning Erich and Germany)—which shows how foreign my behaviour still is to you and how little you understand me! I don't want to discuss this regrettable point of view of yours in detail—I might explode—but would just like to say this: A duty does exist, indeed a very great duty, but it's on the other side. (The "right" and "protection" to which you refer I totally repudiate! A pity you haven't yet managed to get into your head that all the bridges are burnt, inside and out, and that I've got nothing more to do with all that!) And if you really understand me, you'll realise that I am and always have been logical with myself, and that I accept all the consequences precisely because for me there's no other way out. And you can be sure of this: That I know what my duty is towards the party in question—the only duty thinkable to me—and how I must fulfill it. I shall explain everything when you come and then we shall see whether you still have the courage of your eternal compromises. For that's how it is; you're "fifty-fifty" and that's your tragedy. It's what weighs on you like a primeval burden, and if things go wrong with you, and if you suffer, it's because you're "fifty-fifty". Because *whole* people rely on themselves, and the storms and stresses of the world don't touch them because they preserve deep in their hearts something nothing can reach: the will to their own destiny and their own inmost suffering. Enough, enough, we'll talk of this again.

I've just received a letter from Liena after a long long time. Inexpressible joy, redoubled by the realization that we're still very close to each other. You know, it's so beautiful—this love for something to which one no longer lays any claim, this absolutely free emotion, made free through renunciation. When the violences and even the wild griefs of the past dissolve into a pure and deep melancholy, from which new happiness is born.

My darling Mother, all is going well here, so don't worry. But do everything you possibly can so as to get here as soon as possible. And write quickly. I kiss you.

Your Peter

Athens, 23 May 1940

Dearest Mother,

Forgive me for not having answered before. I received your letters and the money, for which a thousand thanks. My position is still unclear because the police haven't yet summoned me. But don't worry —it's a good sign, if anything.

Now there are various matters to discuss:

First, Bruno's card. I'm sending it back to you herewith. I shan't go and see the person he refers me to because, after mature reflection, I feel Palestine doesn't really enter into my view of things at the moment. So don't take any more steps in that direction.

Second, the Brazil plan. I was misinformed; obtaining a visa involves more difficulties than I thought and at the moment they're insurmountable. Not to speak of the fare which I'm not in a position to raise. Your moves in this respect are therefore unnecessary so please don't stir up the world about this money. There's no point.

Third, our disagreement about "the other side". I shall carry things through to the very end, provided only that I'm given the opportunity. It's inaccurate to say, as you do, that the opportunity is open to me *a priori*. On the contrary, the situation such as it is today gives very little hope. But I shall press on as far as is possible because the first formalities are already completed. If you hold it against me that I'm envisaging South America, then here again you are wrong. If I decide to go there it will be because all other exits are closed to me and it's the only remaining solution if I want to avoid another Portugal and the resultant frustrations.

Fourth, your trip. I've been to the Bulgarian Consulate and they have been in touch with the Greek Ministry for Foreign Affairs. The Greek Consulate in Sofia will have to explain why you have not been granted a visa, given that the story of having to put down five thousand leva has never been heard of and is obviously some kind of excuse. It seems probable that at the request of the Bulgarian Consulate an application will be sent asking that you be given free permission to leave as your sole purpose is to visit your son. If the application goes through, you will be discharged of any obligation to put down five thousand leva.

Fifth, Erich's visit. I'm very sorry to have to say so, but it's quite impossible for him to come with you. I can't put things more plainly at the moment, but it's absolutely out of the question, he mustn't come, for my sake. So if you want to await his arrival, then do so, but come alone. It's very serious, Mother, and I absolutely refuse to enter into contact with him. You'll understand later . . .

All other questions and differences by word of mouth. I've a great deal to tell you on very specific matters and I must admit in all honesty that I'm rather sad about your way of thinking. But putting that aside, I am as always with all my love,

Your Peter

Athens, 28 May 1940

Dearest Mother,

Please forgive me any unpleasantness my tactless intervention has caused you, but I really couldn't have guessed it would do you any harm. Anyway, don't worry, nothing has happened yet. The only thing that upset the people here, in an absolutely generalized way, was that business of the five thousand leva and what it signified, because it was the first time, so I was told, that money had ever been demanded for granting a visa. After receiving your telegram I went at once to the Consulate and asked them to stop their efforts as you were now no longer in a position to leave. So everything is in order and you've no need to be alarmed or to fear that I'll behave like that again. In future I'll do only what you tell me. Forgive me, Mother, I merely wanted to make things easier for you. The employee at the Consulate couldn't have been nicer and he said he'd see to everything. So there we are!

Unfortunately things aren't going too well at this end. The Committee has withdrawn its subsidy without giving me any explanation. Of course I know why, but I can't tell you more at the moment. It's depressing to observe the way people think now, and all the pettiness and meanness that exists even among those on "the other side". Because they themselves are no longer in a position to think straight, they take it for granted *a priori* that others proceed by devious means too, and they suspect God knows what shady manoeuvres behind the most straightforward actions. I don't know how I'm going to make out, but to tell the truth I don't think about it much any more because I'm too tired. I'll tell you something, Mother, and that is that you have to be a swine if you want to pull through these days. People who see things as I do don't get far, but what can I do if I've no talent for filth? I really am "touchingly naïve", as someone said of me the other day, but it simply can't be helped, no one will change me.

Now listen, I've got to talk frankly: Either I can hold on here and perhaps even get some work, that's one possibility. The second possibility—but no, it's really the first—would be to get myself accepted as a volunteer in the French or British army. I've been to the two relevant consulates and been enrolled on their lists. In that case I shall probably be sent to Syria, because volunteers aren't accepted for the French front. If I am accepted, I shall leave at once, and that will put an end to all discussion. But if I'm not accepted—which is unfortunately the more likely hypothesis, the way things are — and if I can't hold on here, then two possibilities remain: either Bolivia — in which case as soon as may be and for good — or else Bulgaria, if all other doors are closed and I'm threatened with a repetition of Portugal. But keep calm—it will only be as a last resort, not before. But, you see, I only have to present my German passport, on which as yet the letter "J" has not been stamped, and I am at once granted a Bulgarian visa, and the man at the Consulate told me I could live there for a time provided I didn't work. That's why I beseech you to reconsider the matter (let me repeat: It would only be as a final resort!) and let me know what objective dangers my presence in Sofia would entail if I kept quiet from all points of view. As for the money aspect, I'm sure I would be able to earn what I would cost you by giving lessons or in other ways. Or even more. What I want from you is specific information. I need to know if it's a viable proposition supposing I was forced to leave here suddenly. Imagine that I cross the nearest frontier, we would all be in a fine mess, wouldn't we? For we mustn't deceive ourselves. Everything is very difficult here and you won't really be convinced of it until I can explain the whole situation to you. That's why I press you so urgently to come. With all my love.

Your Peter

Athens, 31 May 1940

Mother, my sweet love,

Oh what a lovely letter I've just received . . . I forbid you to be frightened on my account or to fill your head with such nonsense! Because what you say about feeling you're to blame for what's happening is nonsense from A to Z. I know very well that you're not to blame and have I ever reproached you for anything? No, there's no question of blame here, I'm fully aware of your difficulties, and even if I don't always take account of them in my letters, it's only so as to show a little initiative, for you are always so apprehensive. Oh yes, Mother, you've become terribly easily frightened! But never, never do I lose sight of how tough your situation is. And another thing: We *aren't* quarrelling! If you sometimes answer me back and if I on my side sometimes contradict you, is that quarrelling? And anyway you must remember how anger always used to flare up between us and then die down again: gnashing of teeth at five o'clock with 5,678 grievances, and at five forty-five huge hugs accompanied by assurances that all had long been forgotten! That's how things normally happen between you and me, for we are old hands at fighting!

And as for the love aspect, do you really know how much I love you? No, you certainly don't, because I love you more than sons usually love their mothers, for I don't love you only as a mother, but also . . . how can I put it? . . . but also as, well then, yes, as a woman, there's no other word. But I'm sure you understand, and this doubtless stems from the fact that you are still so young and you and I are almost on the same level. And above all, we are so terribly similar in our innermost depths, similar not like a mother and son but like two friends. Oh God, how to explain if you don't understand . . . For, do you see, where we're closest is in our unreasonableness and our wild impulses . . . It's there that we're most in harmony, in fact totally so. And to be in such harmony you have to be more than mother and son! I'm afraid you won't altogether understand what

I'm saying, but it can't be helped. What you will understand at least is that I love you, infinitely, enough to burst.

You know how grateful I am for your financial help. But it's a great sacrifice for you, so don't send any more, or anyway not so much. Because when all's said and done I'm wasting money here, and things have come right again with the Committee. I don't want you to deprive yourself too much for my sake. I've always got the necessary for food, don't worry! And then you must save up for your trip. I don't ring you up because it costs a fortune and isn't worth it, glorious though it would be. And anyway it won't be long now, will it, before you come?

Do I know people here? Yes, heaps. What I lack is a woman. And it's terribly difficult to find one. By the way today is Liena's birthday. We became engaged two years ago. Moonshine. Of course I haven't received my suitcase and Portugal never answers my letters. Very convenient. No, I don't know Zweig's book. It's probably his book of famous essays, is it? I think I've only read bits of them. At the moment I'm deep in Frank Thiess who is sometimes rather heavy going. I miss my books very much. My darling Mother, I kiss you. And rest assured that nothing could ever come between us that would be strong enough to separate us. Goodbye, dearest Mother.

Your Peter

Athens, 5 June 1940

My darling little Angelika,

Do you know I've had no news from you? Have you been struck dumb? Are you incapable of writing a letter and telling me something about yourself? Or perhaps you think it isn't necessary? How are you, what are you doing, have you quite recovered? Mother told me you weren't going to school, so what do you do from morning till night? To tell you the truth, I can't exactly visualize the life you three are leading together. If only I could appear unexpectedly in your house, in an absolutely mad way (like I used to) and slip my hand over your mouth which would be wide open with astonishment! Just imagine it. Perhaps at dinnertime, when Mother is endlessly moving back and forth, when Tina is telling idiotic stories, and you're sulking because the bread isn't buttered to your liking . . . Yes, if I could appear in the doorway, late as usual, not to have all my incorrigible faults ticked off this time, but to be welcomed with a huge explosion of delight . . . Oh, how marvellous it would be . . .

So write, little donkey, and let me kiss you and tell you I love you.

Your Peter

Athens, 6 June 1940

Darling Mother,

Once again you're worrying for no good reason. By and large my morale is very good, I'm sometimes tired, that's all. It's perfectly natural that I should be depressed now and again for one reason or another and that then I should talk too much about it. But, as you know, I've got a cheerful disposition, depression doesn't last long with me and doesn't undermine my resolution. This remains intact and will continue to do so, all I hope is that I shall be given the chance to show it.

Which doesn't look likely at the moment. What you tell me about Bulgaria surprises me, I must say; I had been given quite a different picture. But if it is as you say then I must naturally exclude that possibility. You're quite right about that. I hope in any case that the situation won't arise of my having to envisage it even as a last resort, because here things are taking a turn for the better. A certain easing-up is apparent, and if I'm not greatly mistaken everything will soon come right.

Tina's behaviour certainly sounds deplorable, but I think you're being over-dramatic about it. She's at the age when adolescents get blinded by their successes, the compliments they receive, the heady awareness of no longer being children (and it's even truer with girls), so they think themselves marvellous and tend to display a surface personality, which doesn't mean that they're really superficial in any basic sense. True self-awareness comes at a later stage, and there's no reason to suppose things will be different with Tina. Nor does her lack of intellectual curiosity strike me as being too heinous. You must remember how young she is. And tell me how you can expect her to have a basic formation when she's never had the chance to be properly educated. You must be fair to her. Let her wallow in her nonsense, let her be silly, it's all in the course of nature.

Goodbye, my darling. I can assure you that for me you're a "fabulous" mother. I'm indescribably glad to have you, I love you with all my soul and kiss you.

Your Peter

Athens, 14 June 1940

Tell me, what's happening, why this silence? It's a week since you've written. I'm worried. Please put my mind at rest at once! And how about the money you told me would be coming? Are you having difficulties? I'm really terribly short and don't know how I'll carry on if I get nothing from you. Forgive me for seeming so pressing, but, as you know, my hands are tied. I can't work—how could I when I'm forbidden to do so? And all contact with the Committee is finished for good. Let me have your news at once and, please, send some money, it's urgent.

Goodbye, I kiss you.

Your Peter

Athens, 22 June 1940

Dearest Mother,

Four letters from you have arrived. You really are odd: I just kick my heels and wait while you send your letters through Germany. What did you hope to achieve when you sent your letter of the 12th to Berlin? Were you absolutely determined that it should be opened and stamped by 578 minor employees? Because that's what happened, so it's all to the good that it was harmless. But do avoid that in future!

By temporarily suspending all granting of visas, the Greeks have at least eliminated one disaster, that of reciprocal reproaches between us two. But still, I'm longing for the suspension to be withdrawn so that finally, finally you can come!

I've had a letter from Grandmother; I too get the impression that she's very well and, everything considered, calm, and this makes me very happy. She has one great advantage over us; the things of war which affect us so intimately don't exist for her. She's no longer in a state to think about them and that's a great good fortune for her. If you ask me what will be the ultimate fate of our people, I can only say that it's my constant anxiety. But oppression has become the rule; the fate of one particular group loses its importance and pales before the enormity of events. Yet I remain an optimist in spite of everything; I believe in the countries that today ought to be believed in. The only trouble is that it may go on for a very, very long time. But the final outcome is certain, you can be sure of that. Write soon, my darling, and please let me know when I can expect the money.

A thousand kisses and all the love of

Your Peter

Athens, 3 July 1940

Dearest Mother,

Thank you for the money which arrived only just in time. The postman had simply mislaid your registered letter! By way of reparation the post office offered to discipline him. To be absolutely honest I had in fact counted on a thousand. Because, you see, it's so terribly difficult here and there's a limit to . . . When one can't go on, one can't go on! Even the smallest contribution makes all the difference to me and I was thinking of asking you if you could possibly let me have five hundred a month. I do assure you, Mother, I wouldn't ask this if I wasn't forced to, because I know how hard things are for you too. But my situation is such—don't let's pretend to each other—that I can no longer indulge the luxury of scruples. I've no choice . . . Like thousands of other emigrants.

Will you ever come? Is it absolutely impossible in the near future? And how about Bolivia? Have you forgotten? Or is there nothing to be done in that quarter?

I'm getting frightened for you again, my darling. The tone of your letters is so desperate! Alas, there's nothing I can answer. But I would at least like to say this: Think of the sufferings of others and then compare them with your own! I would never have thought that it helps but now I know that it does. I kiss you with all my love and don't give up, mind!

Always your Peter

Because, you see, we've got to live. And we can't depend on ourselves any more because our hands are tied. Couldn't we receive a small monthly sum from Rio or America, from Walter Slezak for example? Ten to fifteen dollars, not more. For me it would be terrific and for Walter a mere nothing. Can you write to him, to ask?

Athens, 8 July 1940

Dearest Mother,

I assure you I've got enough for food and lodging and that things are looking up. It's not true at all that I'm at rock bottom. I'm still in one piece and no one like me ever goes under. One has to cling on and hope, that's all. And this I'm doing. Only one thing depresses me: I'm not managing to write, I mean write for myself. Do you think it's some temporary incapacity to do with the circumstances and all these horrors, or am I really incapable of writing? Sometimes I'm terrified that the latter explanation is the true one. And then what? Because it's my only reason for living . . . To take up some "voluntary" work as you suggest is simply not on.

I've tried everything; that's forbidden too. I've already offered my services to the Committee and they told me I hadn't the right to do even voluntary work. But there are little things that help me—you understand. To a slight degree, as in Portugal. Oh yes.

When I told you I'd been hoping for a thousand leva it was a simple statement of fact. I know perfectly well you're doing all you can. I can't understand how you could have detected a hint of reproach in my letter . . . All right, so I'm cross, so I don't love you any more, so I accuse you of not caring about me! Admit, Mother, that you've never thought up anything quite so absurd! Must I tell you again that my gratitude is infinite, like my love? Is it clear?

The heat here is unbearable, much stronger than in Portugal. And I suffer from it considerably. So . . . Uncle Schrobsdorff is with you and you are surely very happy. Enjoy yourself as much as you can. And answer me soon, my darling. A thousand kisses and all my love.

Your Peter

If Walter doesn't answer, we could write to Ernst Lubitsch in Hollywood. He's a friend of Walter's and Walter must certainly have his address.

Athens, 14 August 1940

Dearest Mother,

I'm very well at the moment and hope it will last. It's taken four months, but as you see, everything comes right in the end.

Contrary to what you suppose, the essential question is the one of victory and defeat. It's the only question. And it's only England's victory that counts; I hope for it more ardently than for anything else in the world, I can think of nothing else. The victory of civilization over barbarism, the victory of human values and human dignity over the boot, over an appalling, sickening, limitless tyranny. It's in England, where the fate of the battle will now be decided, that the vanguard of mankind is fighting, and all the admiration I'm capable of pours out to those men over there who are giving everything and who will win because they must win.

As for me, I shall never "back down" as you suggest. To begin with I have an unshakable conviction that our reasons to exist, what we live for, what we believe in—beauty, art, dignity, freedom—will be restored to us as supreme values, in all the glory of their brilliance and nobility, once this ordeal is over. But even if those values were to be destroyed forever, even if I were given proof of their annihilation, I still wouldn't budge; to move an inch towards the "new order" would be to disown my very self, and thus would be impossible. For—and this is where your argument breaks down—age (my supposed youth!) has nothing to do with the matter. Here is one view of life face to face with another view of life, and once we know which view is ours—and for what motives, motives involving our whole being, we have chosen it —then there's no possible retreat. There's only one world I personally can live in, and if it perishes — if there's not even a desert island I can flee to and find solitude — then I perish with it. But the possibility of backing down will never get even the shadow of a thought from me. I will never be tempted to flow with the tide—even taking practical considerations into account, thoughts like "What else can one do?" or "Don't miss the bus." For nothing disgusts me more than people who begin to compromise with the "new" and try to justify its existence for their own miserable ends. And as for the contortionists who think in two languages, I'm "chauvinistic" enough to put all of them into the same sack with the other luminaries and show them my utter contempt! The man who even allows himself to discuss the value of the "new" has already ceased to be one of us. Similarly, the man who flaunts his objectivity like a shield thinking it will protect him. Objectivity is no longer possible, only unconditionality, hate and action!

This is how I see things and, believe me, I'd give a good deal not to have to remain passive but to do what I look on as my duty—that will be my one and final answer to the exploits of those fine German gentlemen.

There I go, once again I've said a lot, perhaps too much, but what the hell . . .

Dearest Mother, my darling, don't be cross because my letter is so late in reaching you. And don't give me any more crap like "eating is more important than sentiments", but come, simply *come*—that's what's *important*! I keep on having to find new rooms because all the landladies here are swine.

I give you a big kiss and am always close to you,

Your Peter

Athens, 7 September 1940

Dearest Mother,

I'm afraid the optimistic forecasts of my letter before last were premature; I'm still stagnating. Things never go as one wants them to and the struggle here is made more difficult by the fact that no one can be trusted. However I hope October will be better and the winter in general more satisfactory.

I've now got an English girl, or to be more exact an

Australian, who couldn't be sweeter and kinder. But she's a virgin, which in itself wouldn't be a tragedy (as it's easy to remedy) if only she weren't a virgin on principle. This obviously complicates things considerably. Perhaps you're familiar with this type of girl. They think this difference they have from other girls (the vast majority) is the most important thing on earth and they safeguard their halo with the most jealous care—an odd mixture of vanity and received ideas. Of course they know they won't keep it for long. That only enhances its value in their eyes.

So my English girl is of this type, and is moreover built in a way that absolutely contradicts all my ideas of feminine beauty and seductiveness. Never mind, I'm putting up a good fight.

Write to me soon, my dear Mother. I give you a huge kiss.

Your Peter

Athens, 18 September 1940

My dear Tina,

Mother told me in her last letter about the unfriendly relations that have developed between the two of you. She wasn't complaining, as you know that's not her style. She was simply giving a very objective description of your relations. I want to say a few words about this, a right granted me by my age—and so my greater ability to judge—or simply by the boundless love and admiration I have for Mother. Or else—enough in itself—by my position as an impartial observer who condemns evil, approves the good and protects the weak against the strong. So I forbid you to torment Mother, or to oppress her, or to make her unhappy or even worried. I forbid you to be thoughtless towards her, to lack respect for her or show her ill-will.

I'm not interested in the reasons for your hostility. The only thing that matters to me is that your current attitude to Mother is an amalgam of cruelty, contempt and the sort of insubordination I know so well. All through stupidity and ignorance. And I'm putting it mildly.

No doubt you will object that I myself had the same complications with her when I was your age. To which I reply, most of our quarrels arose from the clash of two identical temperaments. Passionate, violent, then immediately afterwards becalmed and incapable of rancour; cynical and intolerant one day, and then the next loving and compliant; bursting with spirit and ingenuity in the morning, weary and apathetic in the afternoon. As Mother said one day, she and I are as like as two peas. We were never at a loss for occasions of conflict. But what was my attitude at such times? First and foremost it was respectful, the attitude of an adversary who rages, abuses, lets himself go, yes, but always in the interests of imposing his opinion and never, do you hear, never, through dislike or contempt. That's what "respectful" means. I never felt any resentment against Mother as a person, I never for one moment thought ill of her however violent our crises were. That's why our explosive quarrels always ended in reconciliation and solemn promises to change (which, to tell the truth, didn't last for long), because—and this is what matters—I was always open and disposed to harmony, at her first tender word I would turn round, wanting nothing but to hold her in my arms.

Also, our quarrels were always about my desire for unconditional freedom. Stupid, inept, and unthinking as I was at that time, I misunderstood the word and maliciously altered its meaning to suit my own purposes. We clashed because Mother wanted to make me see reason at a time when I was obviously not yet ready for it. But characteristically I did not want to offend Mother, nor to oppose her just "for the fun of it". Indeed I preferred to go off somewhere and tried by all possible means to avoid the clash. Now, listen: I never attacked Mother because she thought differently from me, but I was at the mercy of my obsession about "my freedom", and so I saw only my own point of view and was concerned with nothing but imposing it . . . And I remember our only *real* quarrel, the one which really did poison us both. I'm not too sure what started it off—I must have been really foul. On the night before my birthday she came into my room and gave me a letter without saying a word. She seemed worried, tortured, and when I saw her like that in her nightdress, so small and frail, I was overcome by such a sense of shame, remorse and love, that after she'd gone out again, and having glanced at her letter, I burst out crying. I wept for a long time, unable to hold back my tears, I vowed a thousand times to reform myself from top to bottom and to be more loving towards her from then on . . .

But at that time — and this is the really important point — Mother was still strong, still overflowing with vitality, initiative, and fight, she resisted, returned blow for blow, and so she suffered much less from our disagreements then than she does from yours now. The war and the upheavals that have come in its train have worn her down; today Mother is at the end of her strength, she has no more reserves to draw on. She needs calm, stability and care and, most of all, she needs protection. She's no longer like before on an equal level with us.

Must I go on, Tina?

So, to return to what I was saying at the beginning of this letter, listen to me, Tina: change your attitude, change it immediately, change it without conditions or discussions. I'm not a person who likes to threaten, but I can assure you that if you don't change very quickly, then you'll have to reckon with me. I don't allow anyone, even my own sister, to make Mother's life more difficult than it already is, I don't allow anyone to throw her into despair. I shall defend her from and against everyone and don't delude yourself that this is impossible just because I'm so far away!

For do you know what your mother is? Let me tell you: she's an exceptional being, a being worthy of admiration and veneration whatever her weaknesses, infinitely good, simple and human, and at the same time with an intelligence, vision, and wisdom without parallel; yes, in every way she's an outstanding woman, generous to the point of self-forgetfulness, with a broad and free spirit, tolerant, attentive to everyone, absolutely without prejudice regarding her children, and loving them, loving them . . . That's what your mother is, and many might envy you for having her. To hurt such a being—be it through obstinacy, narrow-mindedness or stupidity—is distressing in the utmost.

Just think what Mother gives you compared with what she gets from you in return—you should bury yourself underground in shame! And if this type of consideration doesn't touch you, just try to imagine the sort of inhuman horror that may await us and how we shall then have but one recourse: to stand side by side, shoulder to shoulder, so as to transmute our common weakness into strength, to tap from there the courage to defend ourselves; abolishing all that is personal, all pettinesses and vanities, to bring chance onto our side, chance whose name is solidarity, mutual help, kindness, tolerance, the disposition to sacrifice.

This is what I wanted to say to you. And I hope I haven't spoken in vain. If you want to answer, then please do so. You can tell Mother about this letter if you want to. It's up to you.

Your Peter

Athens, 18 September 1940

Dearest Mother,

Many thanks for the photographs and especially for the one of you. It's difficult to make out much and it would be better if your face was in the foreground for once, but anyway I've put it in my wallet and take a furtive look at it from time to time.

I'm very distressed by what you tell me about Tina. I have just written her a long letter — with your tacit consent — but please don't ask to see it if she doesn't show it to you of her own accord. You're not to blame for anything, it's Tina who's in the wrong; you can't explain away her conduct by her youth or by the arrogance that accompanies first love; there's also her tough, obstinate character, what you rightly call her peasant distrust. The truth is that Tina is now a stranger to me, I can't visualize her any more. And any comparison of her with me is no longer helpful; we're totally different and conditions are no longer the same.

So that's that. Don't be too tragic about it, she's still very young, she'll change. You on your side must try to show her a little coldness and contempt; stop showing her excessive love and the desire to make up at all costs. And, most importantly, give her free rein. You can't hold her in, she's stronger than you.

I'm speaking now in an objective and detached way, but at bottom I'm outraged that she should make you suffer, you don't deserve it, it makes me wild. I've written very firmly to Tina and I hope she'll take my words to heart. There's nothing more I can do. If I were home I'd bring her to heel I assure you.

To hear that Angelika is reading *Werther* is as surprising as it is delightful. I have to admit to my great shame that I've never yet come to grips with it, so, you see, she's overtaking me already! How far will she go? As for her "complications," no need for you to worry, she has a strong nature and the tensions within it are not a danger to her, quite the reverse.

Write soon, my darling, I long to hear from you. There's nothing new to report from here. How about the money from America? Has anything been, will anything be, sent? Please keep me informed. All my love, I kiss you.

Your Peter

Athens, 28 October 1940

My darling,

No panic, please, nothing has changed. Of course it's always difficult to see how the situation will evolve, but it's generally assumed that here, where we are, we won't be affected by future developments. Wish for luck! And yet it's possible that contact between us will be interrupted soon. If that occurs, please don't be unduly alarmed; nothing can happen to me, nothing will happen to me. All we can hope is that the outcome will be the one we wish for! Write to me at once, assuming the post still functions. If anything important should develop, I'll try to let you know at once.

I kiss you and hug you a thousand times.

Your Peter

Athens, 23 November 1940

My darling,

Since the declaration of war[22] I've totally lost touch with you. It's true communications were cut off at first, but they're now more or less back to normal and I've been assured that letters are getting through. So why haven't I had any news?

All is calm here and I'm well. But unfortunately I've not been given a job on any front, so I just have to be patient.

I hope all is well with you. Please write and let me know so that I can be sure. I love you and kiss you endlessly. And have courage, you'll see!

Your Peter

[*Undated*]

My beloved,

Imagine my delight—your card dated 25 December arrived on the eve of my birthday! It's consol-

[22]In November, 1940, Bulgaria declared war against England.

ing that there should still be such coincidences for those who love each other! Thank you from the bottom of my heart, my darling, for your words of love and hope. In fact few words are needed to express love when it's deep and strong and your card brings me more than a thousand letters. It's good, it's marvellous to know you're so close, so intimately close to me! Is there an emotion in the world equal to this? I bless you, my darling, if I needed any more strength and reassurance your love has given them to me. You've nothing to fear for me now. I'm protected!

Here it's always the same, except that I've got some good news; at last I've been granted my famous work permit. So I'm searching relentlessly (for work), as it isn't easy to find. But I'll break through in the end and find again my autonomy, my freedom!

Take care of yourself, Mother, my darling. May my love protect you, too.

Peter

Athens, 27 January 1941

Mother, my darling,

I've just this moment received your dear card which has been wandering about for twenty-three days! Perhaps if we sent only stamps things would move quicker.

I'm feeling sad today; it's a long time since I've felt my loneliness so acutely. It came on me suddenly, like a hot wave, for a stupid reason hardly worth mentioning, and yet I've been submerged by it. In the course of the last months—more than a year already!—I've been totally immersed in material cares, and survival has been my sole preoccupation. I've written nothing since Portugal, and though I don't claim to have achieved anything important even then—except in my imagination—at least my powerlessness (accompanied by the agonising awareness of wasted time) was not so obvious then as it is now. The fact that I see things so clearly is a very meagre consolation; my inability to write remains the same. And yet it should be there, it will be there, it must be there, but when, when?

In spite of everything, life goes on. No changes. I'm well, I'm giving lessons. Write to me.

A thousand kisses to the children, and to you my most tender love.

Your Peter

Athens, 17 February 1941

My very darling Mother,

Many, many thanks for your two cards and the ravishing photo of Angelika! How pretty she is! And she's changing more and more into a Lucretia Borgia: angelic and depraved, gentle yet imperious, a sweet and fragile blond beauty allied to an original and devastating spirit. A being apart, a rich and complex personality.

I would have loved so much to watch her grow, day after day. But she has now stopped being a child. How time flies . . .

I'm so pleased, my darling, that you've got friends and that you sometimes have fun. Oh if only I could be with you! What interminable talks we could have—I've got so many words accumulated inside me for you alone! And how indescribably happy we would be, yes, indescribably, I know it. These two and a half years of separation have bound us to each other. I love you beyond all words, my sweet. Tell me, are you all well? Are you all tranquil? Here all is calm, no change. It's warmer, that's all, and I'm longing for the spring.

All my thoughts and all my love. Goodbye.

Your Peter

Athens, 5 March 1941

My darling Mother,

I sent you a telegram yesterday and again I repeat: Don't be worried, don't be alarmed, even if you don't get any news. My silence will be *absolutely* normal. We've got to pass through this period of trial. I'm more confident than I've ever been and I know what I'm doing is right. I'm with you all in my heart, you're all in each and every one of my thoughts. Take care of yourselves, my loved ones, and hold fast. I can only pray for you now and wrap you in such a love that will give you the strength to resist everything.

I kiss you and the children, infinitely.

Peter

Athens, 14 March 1941

Mother darling,

Another attempt to reassure you that all is going for the best. You can be at peace, and remain there, you must! Your telegram arrived safely and I'm delighted at the excellent news it contained. May things go on like that, I wish for nothing else. I am with you and I know that you, too, are with me. The certainty of this gives me strength in my resolution and I thank you, Mother, I thank you for all that you are, all that you are for me: more than a mother . . . something larger, higher . . .

I kiss you.
Peter

With this last letter contact between mother and son comes to an end. Eleven months later Peter's mother received a Red Cross message from Jerusalem. In it Peter told her that he was in Palestine staying with a mutual friend, Ilse Hirsch (who herself had left Berlin in 1936) and that he had chosen to live there. These Red Cross messages, sent very irregularly and arriving very slowly at their destination, remained their sole means of communication throughout the war. And then on 30 June 1945 (her birthday), after the end of hostilities, Peter's mother, still in Sofia, received a letter dated 27 November 1944:

27 November 1944

Mother, Bettina, Angelika, my darlings,

I'm huddled in a tent in the middle of the woods. I'm cold, it's raining, it's autumn, but I've got a blanket wrapped around me. The woods are in France, somewhere on the western front. We're in the front line and opposite us are the Germans. From time to time we can see them about two or three hundred metres away . . . Apart from sporadic gunfire and the thunder of artillery now and again, all is quiet. All is quiet and it's raining and I'm cold, and I'm writing you my first letter for four years.

I agree it's taken me some time to write. When I heard the great news, and when the news was confirmed as true[23] I wrote at once, but then stopped almost as soon. Because it wasn't me who was writing, but another, a stranger. And yet the spirit, the flightiness of impassioned hours has surely always dwelt within me . . .

But now the bird has no wings. I wanted to write a little every day. I tried, I tried to be myself — but I couldn't. Because, you see, four years have passed, because I was and am writing in a language we've never spoken together,[24] because there are so many things to say. They come rushing, dashing upon me all at the same time, they snowball, they collide with each other until I'm thoroughly confused and discouraged; first of all, then, order has to be restored, vision clarified, confusion dissipated, and then contact and warmth have to be rediscovered, as well as a way of expressing myself that doesn't ring false. Because we've become unused to each other, each of us has altered in the course of these four years, years that the others have not lived through. And also because I've changed in many strange ways, and have experienced an incapacity which has long puzzled and tormented me. I've forgotten how to write and even how to talk.

[23]The entry of the Red Army into Sofia, 9 September 1944.

[24]Peter's letter was written in French. But it was a German version subsequently made by the mother for her children and her friends that Angelika gave me. So this is a translation from the German.

It's terrifying how difficult it can be to write a letter, everything is lacking: the calm I need for concentration and ease of expression, and all around there's nothing but obstacles and hindrances. In short, I've become dumb during these war years.

So I've let time pass, as time is needed for everything, and sometimes the right moment comes very late. Perhaps it has come now—I'm writing, I'm writing to you all, I'm writing my first letter . . . To you, my dear Mother, whom I love beyond all words, to whom goes the totality of my love (the homesickness weighs on me like lead!); to you, dear Bettina, who are grown up now, grown far beyond the picture I have of you, become a woman I don't know, a woman I've never seen, a woman my imagination balks at visualizing; to you, dear little Angelika, whom on the other hand I see very clearly, despite your newly acquired seventeen years and although you're doubtless a highly determined and self-assured young woman by now, still I see you, sense you, know how you walk, how you carry yourself, how you look at things, how your grace and charm express themselves, because your character and personality have always been distinctive. Your personal style was already clearly outlined before I left, you were following so straight a path that it's not surprising to think of you now as a complete little person.

So . . . I'm writing at last, but how can I best convey to you what these four years have been, what they have meant in terms of thoughts, sorrows, hopes, disappointments, since we were last in touch, since letters stopped and there were only messages, nothing but messages granted us by a cruel world through the mediation of an international charitable organization. Those messages—twenty-five words at the most—which reached us with a slowness beyond description and after appalling delays. And yet they were all we had, they were our life, our hope, awaited with impatience and anguish as one awaits a verdict—twenty-five miserable words into which we tried to cram a whole world of meaning, an infinity of emotion, an excess of reassurance. How can I describe how long and agonising and unendurable this separation has been for me; how month has followed month, and month piled up on month, without the end coming any nearer; how the years have dragged by heavy with tedium and homesickness; how the hope the war would end became more and more obsessive; how can I explain, Mother, all that's gone on inside me: my anxiety, my anguish, all the times when I didn't know where you were, my constant longing to help you, to give you support, to run to you if you needed me, all the while knowing, alas, it was impossible; all my love which I wrapped round you as if to protect you, all my hope that I would live to see the day when this way of life would change, when hostilities would end, when I would get in touch with you all again in a normal way and when—blissful thought—I would see you!

Well, that time has now come! Not the great day itself, but the first day, the beginning of the end, the getting in touch with you again. I was in a small French village when I heard people saying, "Our Russian allies have entered Bulgaria and are rapidly advancing." What news! What glorious news! Mother, I was mad with joy! Then I calmed down a bit and examined the information in all its aspects. It wasn't certain yet. I awaited further news with an impatience I can't begin to describe. Some days later it came: Sofia was liberated! You were outside the criminal ring, you were in our world. Free, yes free; free to speak and receive the truth, free from the oppression you had originally fled but which caught up with you as you were living in an "Axis" country, given over to intellectual servitude (worse than physical violence), to incessant harassment, to the constant threats of an arbitrary and omnipresent power which made your life increasingly precarious and dangerous; finally, free to speak, to speak to me and to hear me ... But doubts, questions and uncertainties are now crowding in on me: Are you all right? Are you still all together? And still in the same place? Where is each of you? What has the new constellation of events brought to each of you? Who has Bettina married, what kind of man, and what has he been doing during these years? What are you living on, and how? Are you free from want? Can you communicate with me freely and at once? Can we exchange telegrams, letters, etc.? I've only been able to glean very meagre information about your material conditions, very vague indeed, but not actually disquieting. But that makes it no less vital that you should tell me everything at once, as a first priority!

And now, Mother, I think I must tell you a little about what's been happening to me. So I'll begin with what you already knew before the stage was plunged into darkness ...

You knew that ever since the beginning of the war I'd been making innumerable overtures with the idea of enlisting in the Allied armies. And you knew what led me to this decision, which was no more than a natural and logical consequence of my attitudes, unshakable attitudes whose clear and unambiguous conclusions I never hesitated to draw when necessary. No need, then, to hark back to that. You knew my ideas and my way of seeing things, you also knew that at the time of losing contact I had not yet managed to enlist in the British army due to its very stringent regulations forbidding the admission of foreigners — with the exception of those living in Palestine or in England itself. You knew all this because I told you at various times about the steps I was taking and the difficulties I was encountering—which, as I remember, aroused your anxiety because, as you said, I was "too outspoken and not discreet enough".

What you didn't know, but which I'm sure you guessed[25]was that my efforts finally bore fruit.

In December, 1940, I was taken on for the duration of the war as a foreign volunteer with General de Gaulle's Free French Forces — that army, which was tiny at the time, which rejected the armistice and went on with the war side by side with the English. After my acceptance, plus several months of waiting, I was sent at the end of March, 1941, to Egypt, where I became a soldier.

So I've been fighting — and it's not yet over — for more than three and a half years, in all the theatres of the war: in Syria against the Vichy army from May to July, 1941 (at that time I was still a "greenhorn", a young recruit, and had everything to learn); then in Libya—from January to June, 1942—the desert, sand, for long months, thwarted on all fronts, first from one side, then from the other, an eternal monotony, first an advance, then a retreat, then the defence of Tobruk which ended with the fall of Bir-Hakeim. A fortnight's resistance on a small stretch of sand indistinguishable from the rest of the desert, in appalling heat, almost without food, at first with very little water and then with none, under constant bombardment which slowly destroyed the whole position. Then the withdrawal at night of the last survivors under fire from the "Lords" of the Afrika Korps; then Libya again, and then Tunisia. From October, 1942 to May, 1943, more of the desert—which we knew so well by now, with its leaden heat, its cold

[25]See below, the note on p. 130.

nights beneath a vast sky, its wind, its sandstorms, its desperate yet sometimes grandoise monotony—the El-Alamein battle, Montgomery's thrust, the great offensive, sustained, implacable: Tobruk, Derna, Benghazi, Tripoli. Then a moment of peace near Tripoli, that city of trees, greenness, and farms, and our drunken delight at the sight of vegetation and luxuriance after so much aridity. Then forward again, the Mareth line, a different landscape, olive groves as far as the eye could see, mountains, towns. Then the battle of Cape Bon, Tunis. Here, another pause. After some comings and goings we left the English 8th army with which we had fought up till now, that desert army of which Churchill said, "If anyone asks where you fought, just say I was with the 8th army, that's enough!" And then with fresh French reinforcements — involving various changes, but of another kind — we stayed for several months in a small village about ten kilometres from Tunis . . .

Then, the Italian campaign from May to July of this year, the arrival in Naples, the storming of the Gustav line, the thrust across the Hitler line and the great advance right to the north of Rome—I didn't take part in this because I'd been wounded on 16 May during an attack—a slight wound, a bullet in the left shoulder, no complications, total recovery. I spent some weeks in a hospital in the American sector, so was prevented from revisiting Rome, to my bitter disappointment—I had got to know it and love it so much on my journey across Italy on the way to Greece . . .

And finally France: the great event so long awaited, so ardently desired, the great invasion, the disembarkation on the Côte d'Azur on 16 August, the battles in the direction of Toulon and then in front of Toulon, the pursuit along the valley of the Rhône, through countless towns and villages of Provence, of

Lyonnais, of Burgundy, Aix-en-Provence, Arles, Nimes, Saint-Etienne, Lyon, Chalon-sur-Saône; and then again "somewhere in France", the front, attacks, counter-attacks, patrols, night watches, villages razed to the ground, woods, rain, cold, and on it goes . . .

But the end is near. Germany lies before us, not far off, we'll soon be there . . . It doesn't matter what they do, the barbarians—resist to the last man, hold us here and there, now and then—it won't save them! They're on their last gasp and *our* strength is always growing. The pond is drying up mercilessly—Holland, Luxembourg, Lorraine, Alsace, the Alps as far as Mentone, Memel, East Prussia, Warsaw, Czechoslovakia, Budapest, Yugoslavia, and as far as Greece . . .

Thirteen capitals have been snatched from them in a few months—Rome, Paris, Luxembourg, Brussels, Helsinki, Reval, Riga, Kovno, Bucharest, Sofia, Belgrade, Athens, and now Budapest. The first large German city, Aachen, is in our hands. Our air attacks grow stronger day by day . . . Yes, they will be crushed, they will be extinguished if necessary, one town after another; justice will be done. Mankind will have its revenge, it will recover its rights. And the Nazis shall suffer as they have made others suffer, and those who aren't Nazis shall suffer too! For they are all responsible, they are all guilty, except a few, except a tiny minority who chose exile and the struggle for a just cause, or who were unable to flee yet never played the wretched game but resisted all temptation and kept their hands clean. But all the others will pay and pay dear, for they wanted it to be like this, and the day of reckoning is at hand. And also at hand is our liberation, the end of this dog's life, for making war is a dog's life . . . Believe me, it isn't fun at all in the long run and I personally have had enough of it. I've done what I could and a lot more besides. It's time it ended and we returned to a rational way of life. When it drags on it's just no good . . . Yes, a few more weeks perhaps, even a few more months, I willingly accept that. And what I want most of all: to enter Berlin! For my satisfaction, for my vengeance, so that they can see that I was right! I don't know whether this will be possible, perhaps not, but I want to be there at the precise hour, at the precise moment when the reckoning is made. Then I shall go away again, and never return. You mustn't think, Mother, that I have any regrets. I regret the time that has been wasted, all the years that have been stolen from me and that it won't be easy to make up for, because I'm now nearly thirty. But I don't at all regret having done what I did, it was simply my duty, my duty as a free man for whom certain principles are elementary and the very basis of life. I wouldn't have been able to live with my conscience had I hesitated. It was my duty to take up your defence and contribute to your victory. But we'll discuss all this again, I can't say everything in a first letter . . .

And now I want to tell you about Ilse and Walter, our rediscovered friends, and my best and dearest friends. It was in the autumn of 1941, after the Syrian campaign, that I first saw them again. I had finally succeeded in finding their address in Jerusalem — all rather complicated as I thought they lived in Tel Aviv —and had entered into correspondence with them. Then one fine day I knocked at their door. Ilse opened it, let out her famous cry, and we rushed into each other's arms, wild with joy, inexpressibly happy . . . From that moment their house became mine. I spent all my leave with them. And the good old times came back. True friends who you know through and through, long talks where you can say exactly what you like, where there's total reciprocity, where no shade of meaning is too subtle, where prejudices are acknowledged and judgments kind. Light and happy conversation with no dead moments, full of warmth and goodwill; links deriving from so many common interests and experiences; a similar life style, a similar outlook, that close kinship between people of the same blood . . . And so many memories to share! As you know, I was always very fond of Ilse, and we spent the most marvellous hours together. And a true friendship developed between myself and Walter and he helped me over and over again to see things in their true colours. He fought against my innate tendency to manufacture doubts and exaggerated scruples.

It's now over a year since I saw them last and God knows when I shall see them again. In Africa it was easy, I could often get to Palestine. But now from here, from Europe, it's not the same. They're far away now . . .

As for Liena, well, I haven't forgotten her. My commitment to her was so strong that after more than six years and in spite of everything she's still very much alive in my heart. Her image remains whole and intact, ineffaceable, indestructible, not just conjured up intellectually but—how shall I put it?—almost essential, real, present, omnipresent. I can still lose myself and then rediscover myself in her, only in her if truth be told, although I'm so surely and definitively detached from her. If I can talk on another level, I move and have my being with her somewhere where everything expands, dilates in the infinite and universal and where she becomes herself in some impersonal way. It's difficult to explain but perhaps you'll understand. I hope to see her again, *I shall* see her again.

And I'll see others too—my father, for instance. But I'm not thinking about that yet, I don't want to think about it yet, I forbid myself this sort of anticipation. I don't like groping in the dark. I know nothing about him. We shall see.

And now tell me about Grandmother. Is she still

alive? And if so, where is she? I've already asked you this question once and you gave me the laconic reply: "No news for a year." I couldn't pursue the point in my brief messages, but now I shall: How is it possible that you haven't had any news? And, more important, how is it possible that you left her there all alone, abandoned her, knowing full well what it would mean? Had she been deported like the others? Couldn't you really have got hold of her, taken her to you? "No news"! But, good God, you managed to get away, all three of you, and she, poor old woman, had to stay there alone, with no help, perhaps with no money. I can't understand it. When I think she has met the same fate as so many others and that it could have been avoided, I go mad!

And you see, Mother, what they've done to our own people, to all the Jews who hadn't a chance to get away—what they've done to them in the Polish camps and in the ghettos! What those Huns have done, those Germans, those representatives of their people, men from every class, from the north and the south, of every complexion and character! How they've tortured, massacred, systematically exterminated, coldly annihilated! It demands the most terrible vengeance. Those responsible for these atrocities will be judged. But who is responsible? The nation whence such creatures emerged; the spirit and blood of this nation; the human community which allowed such things to exist, to live, to grow, to act, to flourish.

Who is responsible? The nation, of course, which gives itself such leaders, perfect representatives of the general vileness, and which chooses them because it recognises itself in them. Yes, they have all recognised themselves: the killers, the assassins of Lublin and the gas chambers, the thousands of killers who coldly shot, mowed down, gassed, buried alive, burnt alive; the populace who followed or preceded the killers, the populace who broke windows, pillaged houses, ill-treated, humiliated, beat up; and then those who didn't know, who didn't want to know, who let things take their course, who chastely lowered their eyelids while they washed their hands; and finally the mass, the great indifferent mass of "decent chaps", indifferent to the ignominy, the outrage, the radical and irreparable evil that was being done to other men.

Yes, a whole people is to blame, to blame because of its mentality, its spiritual attitude, its indolence, its apathy, its contempt for true civilisation, its inability to control its instincts, its innate barbarism, sometimes hidden and sometimes unleashed and which turns a German into a Hun. If Hitler had been dealing with honest men he would have remained what he was—a charlatan. But he knew who he was singing his dirty songs for, and we know too—for the dirty *Boches;* and they responded in chorus and in unison because he touched them in the depths of their souls, he touched them where they were evil and terrible, where his call awakened a thousand echoes . . .

I must stop. This letter has been written over several days and with many interruptions. I began it under rain, near a stove, went on with it during a few precious hours of peace and warmth, and now am finishing it under snow. We have attacked and are now occupying a new position at an altitude of seven hundred metres. It's cold, cold, cold. We live in holes scooped out of the snow and it's a real feat to write with such numbed and frozen hands. How I regret leaving the hot cities of the East and of Africa, following one after another along the shores of the Mediterranean, landmarks in my war: Beirut, Damascus, Tripoli, Sfax, Sousse, Tunis, Algiers, Casablanca. But no, I regret nothing; because now I'm nearer than ever to you. The war is coming to an end and soon I'll descend from my snowy throne. Meanwhile I've been able to write you a long letter, and that's quite an achievement. Oh Mother, I feel it can't last much longer now, I'm sure I'll see you soon, very soon, you and Bettina and Angelika. What else can I say? How can I speak of things that fill me with such inexpressible happiness, like a great warm wave? Everything inside me is expectation, love . . .

Take care of yourselves, my loved ones, and wait just a little while longer. You're safe now. I needn't worry any more, need I? Tell me, Mother, that I needn't worry! Write at once! Tell me everything! I know so little about you . . .

Goodbye for the moment, my dear ones. I say goodbye for the moment because it surely won't be long now, it can't be long now. We've held out for years, we've held out well, but now it really must stop. Goodbye for the moment, my dearest ones, everything is bathed in huge hope . . .

I love you, I kiss you all over and over again
You, Mother
You, Bettina,
You, Angelika
Peter

Peter Schwiefert was killed in Alsace, two kilometres from the Rhine, on 7 January 1945, about five weeks after sending the above letter. By the time his mother received this letter he had already been dead for six months. She did not know this. She answered it the next day.

Sofia, 1 July 1945

Peter, my little Peter, I can't write to you in the sort of French I would like. It's so difficult to tell you all my love in a language that isn't my own. If only I could speak French as well as you!

Listen—yesterday morning, 30 June, I was in bed, I was daydreaming and I was thinking that if someone came and asked me what I'd like best for my birthday, I would say, a letter from Peter. An hour later there was a ring at the bell and the postman brought me your long letter, the first for four years!

Never have I received such a beautiful and moving letter! I'm wild with love and admiration and longing. I felt, you are my son, you belong entirely to me. You think my thoughts, feel my feelings, speak my language. I love my daughters as much as you, but they are of another kind. I'm afraid they don't love me any more, as you do, and they don't understand me as you understand me. They're always in revolt. Bettina is always against me, or perhaps she's like that just to frustrate me. You know her, she has hardened herself so as never to show her soft heart. Angelika is a severe critic and sometimes she's right. In any case they're both very different from me, different in their inmost being, in their temperament, in their outlook on life. They have no respect for me and I'm often the object of their sarcasm. They get angry, and rightly, when I shout and lose my temper. As you know, that's always been my great fault. I often shouted at you. And I regret every word that wasn't a word of love. That I should be irritable nowadays can perhaps be understood and forgiven. But even in the past when we were all together, when I had all my children around me, and my friends, and my music, and my books, and there were no worries, even then I was often bad-tempered, irritable, ungrateful when I should have been happy, kind and grateful to all of you. And that has to be paid for, my little Peter, and it's only fair that it should be. I behaved badly, selfishly, I neglected my duties even towards my children though I loved them so much. Why am I telling you all this? Because after receiving your letter I want to ask your forgiveness, my dear Peter. Because I'm afraid you love me too much and I don't deserve it. Because when I think about the past I see only my faults, and it tortures me.

That's that. Now I want to talk about you. You've become a man now, you've suffered more than me, you've shown that you knew not only how to write fine phrases but how to risk your life for an ideal. And you've proved your immense attachment to your mother and your grandparents who loved us so much. How small I feel beside them and you! I can't explain everything in this letter. We shall have a long talk about all these things later, shan't we, my little Peter?

I've had a letter from Ilse saying that the last communication she had from you was a telegram from Paris. It said that you wanted to get me to Jerusalem so that we could see each other. Since then she's had no news and nor have I. We are so terribly frightened! I've sent you endless letters and cards through the French and English Consulates—I didn't know where you were, I thought you were still in Jerusalem or Syria. I had your military address, but knew nothing.[1] But now

[1]Peter's Red Cross messages were always sent from Jerusalem. They were written either by Peter himself (when he was there on leave), or, more often, by Ilse Hirsch, or again they were typewritten. And his mother answered to Ilse's. So contrary to what Peter thought (see p. 121) she had never realised that he was in the armed forces. It was not until March, 1945, that Ilse—worried about Peter's silence, and communication with Bulgaria having been re-established—wrote to the mother for the first time. She told her that Peter was a soldier and gave her his military address, otherwise she tried to be vague so as not to alarm her. It was from this time that the mother tried by all possible means to enter into communication with her son.

I know! God spared me four years of anguish and torment. But why haven't we had any news of you for six months? You had been through so much danger, you'd been wounded, and yet you wrote. Now that the war is over, you are silent. But the war went on from November to May. I'm so frightened, Peter!

So you never realised what they did to Grandmother? They deported her to Poland, like all the others, and we've had no news of her since 1943. The first to go were Marie and Evchen. Then all the others—the Habermanns, the Hirsches, all. Ernst Saulman and his mother committed suicide, and many others did the same. Your father helped as much as he could, he kept his hands clean. You don't mention Erich, and I know quite well why. But he was very good to Grandmother and to all of us.

You shower me with reproaches about Grandmother, but, Peter, I couldn't have brought her here. It was out of the question. I myself was only able to leave Germany, as you know, because I contracted a marriage of convenience. We hadn't any passports and in no circumstances would they have let my mother leave. But what's the use of talking about it now, Peter? I shall never understand how such things were able to happen. I shall never understand men. The guilty will be punished, they must pay the price, but even if there were a punishment equal to the measure of their crimes it will not bring the dead back to life.

You can't think how often I've pictured the end of the war to myself, the end of the Nazis. And now to my amazement it has actually come, just as I dreamed of it and longed for it with all my being. I always firmly believed it would come, and yet I sometimes doubted, because it's so seldom that reality ever corresponds to our wild expectations! Like you, I've dreamed of revenge. I wanted to take revenge on everyone who had hurt me, humiliated me, taken everything away from me — my son, my mother, my husband, my country — everyone who'd made my children unhappy and made me make them unhappy, my children whom I love more than the whole world. I minded that most. Yet in spite of everything, I now want to fight against my desire for revenge, I don't want to hate any more. What I would like is to work in my fatherland[2] with the Allies, and for them. I know the country, the language, I've learnt how to work, how to live cheaply, how to want nothing but a little peace and quiet. I ask for one thing only: not to have to be frightened any more and not to have to live alone in a foreign country. And first and foremost I want to have my three children safe and sound and happy and out of danger. I'd like to have them with me, it's the prayer I say night and morning.

My darling Peter, I take you in my arms, I hold you to me, I'm proud of you, my little one.

Mother

The children kiss you. Angelika wants you to come. Will you come, Peter? Sometimes I just can't go on. It was all too much. I see nothing but darkness. If only you could come . . .

His mother learned the news of her son's death a fortnight later, through a letter from Ilse Hirsch dated

[2]Peter's mother uses the word *patrie* here. Compare with the letter to Enie Schwiefert, 3 August 1948, p. 162.

12 June. Ilse had just received the following communication, a belated reply to the enquiries she had initiated. She enclosed a copy of it with her letter.

12 June 1945

Madame,

As a result of this unit's constant movements I have not been able to answer your letter until today—your letter which was passed on to me by Pierre Schwiefert's Company Commander. I do not know what relation you are to our comrade, but on the supposition that you may be in correspondence with his parents, I would ask you to be so good as to inform them of the tragic news of our comrade's death. Pierre Schwiefert was killed on 7 January by shell fire near the Alsatian village of Rossfeld. His company was opposing the Germans who were trying to advance on Strasbourg by breaking through the line of defence that our Brigade was holding between the Rhine on the east and the river Ill on the west.

Pierre was in position in a trench when the shell burst just beside him. He was killed instantly. I saw his body and his face was not disfigured.

Young Schwiefert was a veteran of the Battalion, a very brave and good comrade. I had already known him in Beirut. He had made various moves to see his family—in Bulgaria, I think—and was very happy about going back to Palestine. Alas, God allowed him to be taken from us. I am certain that God will have given this young man his reward; he fought valiantly for his ideal from the time he left Berlin right up to his death.

Please accept my most respectful greetings, Madame, and convey my heartfelt condolences to his family.

Jean Starcky
Captain chaplain of *BIMP*
(Bataillon d'Infanterie de Marine et du Pacifique)[3]

PS Pierre Schwiefert is buried in the military cemetery of Chatenois in Alsace.[4] His belongings may be claimed from the Military Estates Service, 22 boulevard de la Bastille, Paris, 12e.

[3]Peter belonged to the 3rd company of the BIMP, a unit that was formed after Bir-Hakeim by amalgamating the Bataillon du Pacifique with one Bataillon d'Infanterie de Marine (to which Peter had previously belonged). Both battalions had suffered heavy losses.

[4]Peter's body has since been moved. Notification of this was sent to Bettina from the Ministère des Anciens Combattants et Victimes de Guerre (Ministry for ex-Service Men and War Victims) in a letter dated 10 February 1972. The text ran as follows: "Madame, you have expressed a desire to know the burial place of your brother, the soldier Peter Schwiefert, born in Berlin on 5 January 1917 . . . I have the honour to inform you that the mortal remains of this soldier who "died for France" on 7 January 1945 in the Benfeld region (Lower Rhine) repose in the military cemetery of Strasbourg-Kronenburg (Lower Rhine), grave number 24, row 5, section E. Please accept . . . " Signed: illegible, director of the Office of National Cemeteries and the Restitution of Bodies (Bureau des Nécropoles nationales et des Restitutions de Corps).

A few months ago Angelika and I went to Strasbourg-Kronenburg, where we duly found Peter's grave. At the head of the grave was a cross, and the identity disc affixed to it was incorrectly spelled: *Schwerrert* instead of *Schwiefert*. We did what was necessary regarding both the spelling and the cross.—C.L.

From Peter's mother to Ilse Hirsch
Sofia, 17 July 1945

Dear Ils' chen,[5]

Thank you for everything. A hope is dead. My little one whom I was going to see at last. He endured great suffering for seven years and survived four years of extreme danger only to fall at the last moment, four months before the end. I seemed already to feel the touch of his hand, his hair, his face; I'll soon have the whole of him in my arms, I said to myself, I'll be covering him with kisses. But now there's no more Peterlein.

I envy you so much. You had him in your home, you talked to him. I have nothing. And as I hadn't seen him for seven years, physically nothing is changed, everything is as it was before. Only there's now a huge emptiness at the centre of my thoughts, and absolutely no hope. My son was so beautiful, so gifted. I wanted to live with him.

You're the only person I can say these things to because at the moment you're closer to me than anyone. I want to see you, to touch you, because there's still a little of Peter on you. He walked about in your rooms. Ils'chen, tell me about him if you can spare the time, tell me everything you can, everything—describe him to me, was he cheerful, did he have girls, a girl, did he love one particularly? Have you a photograph of him? Send anything you can find, please, please, Ils'chen. (Your letters have arrived safely, but even so don't send lots of things at once, send the less important things first, and if those arrive, send me the rest bit by bit. As for the things he had on him when he was

[5]Ils'chen, Peterlein: affectionate diminutives for Ilse and Peter.

killed, they had better go to you in Jerusalem, if it's impossible to have them sent direct here to the French Legation. I'll talk again about this.)

What do you mean by "his superb appearance"? Please give me a detailed description of how he looked. I feel so bitter when so many have survived; why not him? He didn't deserve it. Did he talk about it? Did he have a premonition that something might happen to him? Was he happy? I feel such remorse. I used to quarrel with him so often. Did he ever say anything against me? Did he feel resentment? For instance because I never managed to get to Greece? He went to meet me at the airport once, and I would perhaps have gone if I had been more energetic. But I was so uncertain and tormented about the children.[6] If only I could have seen him just once again. But, you know, I never really felt frightened for Peter. Except just recently in these past weeks, I felt so empty. Was he often unhappy? Did he worry? You have lost him too, but it doesn't hurt you as it does me. Children always have a bond with their mother even when they're grown up, they're joined to her as if the umbilical cord were still there. And consciously or unconsciously you feel them pulling and pulling, and it breaks your heart. My mother lost her son during the last week of the First World War — I was twenty-three at the time. My best friend was killed on almost the last day. I really don't know how I'm going to survive.

My son had already been dead for six months and I didn't know. Two days after his birthday![7] It had never occurred to me that Peterlein could die in the war. It seems absurd to start crying six months too late as I'm

[6]See below, the letter to Bruno Kirschner of 1 April 1940, p. 154.
[7]Peter was born on 5 January 1917 and died on 7 January 1945.

doing. He had no one with him, his *Mutti*[8] wasn't with him. I'm just no good, no good at all. I never bring anything but disaster. Ils'chen, write to me, and accept my love.

What language did you speak in? How much time did he spend with you in Jerusalem? Did he live with you? What uniform did he wear? How much leave did he have? So he didn't receive my letters and postcards etc.![9] He only received the mail sent through the Red Cross! What can he have thought of me? I didn't write often enough and he was so afraid for us.

Did you know already that Peterlein was dead? Were you trying to prepare me for it? Why did he love me? I've never done anything for him. In my reply to his long letter I told him for the first time how much I loved him, how much I esteemed him and admired him, how much I thanked him and asked his forgiveness for so many things. But he will never know. He died without knowing how much I loved him.

Your "Schnuff"

From Ilse Hirsch to Peter's mother
Jerusalem, 1 August 1945

My dear Else,[10]

I'm going to try to answer your questions as fully as I can.

[8]Mutti, German for "Mommy", mother.
[9]See p. 130.
[10]Peter's mother's given name. She was born Else Kirschner. It should not be confused with Ilse.

And to begin with, no, I knew nothing! Peter had been an irregular correspondent all these years, and especially so towards the end. Last January he sent a telegram announcing his arrival here. And then there was silence. But I didn't start worrying or suspecting anything for several weeks. And even then I still hoped he was only wounded. He had received a bullet in his shoulder at the same time the year before and he had been cared for in an American hospital. And for a long time then I had no news of him.

But let me tell you about him. He was always very gay with me and often said we had our heads full of nothing but nonsense. The first time he arrived at our home on leave he'd been fighting for months on end in the desert, in the most gruelling conditions. I shall never forget the first meal we had together. We had meat, vegetables, and salad and I had stupidly neglected to use the salad bowl. Peter sat down, scrutinized the table, and asked in a voice full of reproach, "Do you mean to say there's no salad bowl here?" It was so typical of him. The minute he arrived he became the spoilt little boy who had to have at least ten servants around him. He took possession of our maid. Whenever he went out his uniform had to be carefully pressed and his shoes polished. He was, quite simply, gorgeous. I've never seen such a handsome man: very pure features, a thick mass of chestnut hair, a magnificent figure. In the street everyone turned round to look at him. He had a girl in every port, everywhere "the most beautiful in the village" as he said, but he didn't love any of them. Over these last years he maintained that I was the only woman he loved. But I knew very well he only loved you, and that he latched onto me because of your and my old friendship. So I tried as it were to get this infatuation out of his head, which rather irritated him at first, but he declared that he hoped to convince me of the reality of his love once the war was over.

No, he never doubted for a moment that he would emerge from the war safe and sound. I used to write to him saying that we would never see each other again, because I assumed he would go to America after the war. And he always wrote back, "Don't you believe it, my dear little Ilse, I'll be with you again soon, very soon."

As for the reunion with you, I can't tell you how many times he pictured it! He always had your photograph on him, and ones of his sisters. He loved you very much, Else. Not only as a mother, but as a woman too; you were extremely vivid and present to him. He always said that you and he were very much alike and he thought when you saw each other again there would be huge discussions followed by a true and very close understanding. To start with, he was absolutely determined to know what your position was on basic problems (and also that of his sisters and Bettina's husband). And equally what you thought about the question of Jew, non-Jew, etc. He tried desperately to become entirely Jewish but without success. An authorization from the military authorities was required for an "operation" and it was refused. The matter was an obsession with him.

He wanted to go to America after the war, become a writer and a journalist and visit Palestine as often as possible. He wasn't a Zionist but he loved Palestine. It was his fatherland. He observed all the Jewish feasts (he even claimed special leave for them), read the Torah, and though he wasn't pious he had infinite respect for the religion. An unceasing conflict raged inside him regarding his father, and nearly tore him in two; he wondered in agony what he would do if by chance he met him. But his hatred of the Germans was so strong that after having thought about it he no longer had any doubts.

We always spoke German together, Peter and I, but we wrote to each other in English. With my children he stammered a little Hebrew. He stayed in Jerusalem once for three weeks and another time for six weeks. Of course he lived with us when he was here and he was always in very good spirits, like at Pätz.[11] He wore the khaki uniform of the Free French Forces with the little navy blue forage cap on the side of his head. As I've already told you, he was marvellously handsome and well-groomed. Besides that, he had wonderful hands. Peter also spent three days with my parents in Tel Aviv. My parents were proud of him and spoilt him terribly.

He received only one letter from you, right at the end. He was mad with joy and wrote to tell me how happy he was.[12] He was terribly frightened for you and wanted to get you to Palestine at all costs. I was to obtain the visas. My letter of reply saying that this

[11]The place near Berlin where the Schrobsdorffs' country house was.

[12]In September, 1944, after the liberation of Sofia, and at more or less the same time as Peter was starting his long letter to her, Else for her part had sent a letter to her son. This is the letter to which Ilse refers here. Peter must have received it only a few days after despatching his own of 27 November; he speaks of it to Ilse in one of the last notes he sent her, 8 December 1944 (see p. 173). Unfortunately, as I explain below, this letter from Else, like all the others Peter received from her, has not been preserved. Angelika, who had read it and added a postscript of her own, recalls that their mother referred in it to her worry that Peter would be shocked

would be impossible[13] would certainly never have reached him. Poor little Peter!

This will have to do for today, Else. My eyes are drooping with exhaustion. Everyone here feels so deeply about Peter's tragic end. But it's done me good to talk to you.

On 24 December last year, Peter was on leave in Paris. He wrote me from there saying that if he didn't have to return at once to the front he would come to Palestine just as soon as possible. On 3 January I received a telegram saying he was just about to leave France and that he was determined to get you to Jerusalem. The explanatory letter arrived on 15 January. All seemed to be going well. Meanwhile there had been the offensive[14]...

In fact I'm always waiting for news of his arrival ... I just can't believe he's gone. He still had so much to do! As I write I'm looking at a photograph of him on the wall opposite.

Write to me, Else, and then I'll write to you more fully about him.

Ilse

---

when he saw her again; she told him she had lost her beauty, that she was going gray, that her face was disfigured by the paralysis of a facial nerve. She also told him of Bettina's marriage, of the probable death of her own mother, but most of all she asked an infinitude of questions about Peter's life—or what she imagined to be his life—in Jerusalem.

[13]Because of the restrictions on Jewish immigration imposed by the British.

[14]The final German offensive of January, 1945, in the course of which Peter Schwiefert was killed.

From Else to her first husband,
Fritz Schwiefert, Peter's father
Sofia, 15 July 1946

Dear Pitt,[15]

Many thanks for your dear letter; if it had arrived earlier it could have helped me.[16] It took a long time for me to realise what was so appallingly agonizing in Peter's death, over and above the knowledge that I would never see him again. It racked me, tormented me, but I was far too disturbed and helpless to explore this thought to the end. Yet you have understood my feeling and expressed it clearly and beautifully—as only you know how.

It wasn't an ordinary kind of loss as when a dear friend dies. There was no illness. No death. There was nothing. A void—no Peter before, no Peter now. I didn't look after him again, protect him again, caress him again, love him again; simply, there is no more Peter. Is it possible? That's what tortured me so relentlessly. No more Peter! Like you, I look for a trace, I look for it like a dog because I'm his mother. If only I knew how sweet his hands and hair were to the touch, if only I'd been able to kiss his lips once again, savour his skin, his odour, his warmth just once more. I look at his photograph, there should be something of Peter in it. But it's cold, and it's sentimental to do it. He won't come back. If I could cry, really cry . . . but I can't. When I face the stark irremediableness of the thing, it hurts too much, so I stop thinking, I don't think about it any more. I'm much the same in front of other people

[15]Fritz Schwiefert's pet name.
[16]Fritz Schwiefert had been informed of his son's death by Erich Schrobsdorff, at a somewhat late date. See below, p. 164.

and I don't wear black. What's the use? Explain to me too why I don't die of it. I should have died a long time ago, it was too much. Am I completely numb, or didn't I love him enough, or is it the instinct for self-preservation? For if I let myself go I know I would howl, howl . . . But that's just it, I don't howl. When my mother lost her son she cried night and day for months. It would make things easier, I think. It stifles you, it stifles you!

But the worst thing isn't that Peter no longer exists for *us*; it's that he no longer exists for himself. He's got nothing at all now, all has been for nothing. He suffered, desired, hoped, for nothing, and even the love he showed us by sacrificing himself we can't repay him. He wanted to start to live. He loved warmth, the summer, girls; he had nothing. You'll understand what I mean when you read his letter, the first and the last I received from him in those four years. It arrived on 30 June of last year, and it was my birthday. What a birthday present, Pitt! But by then it was already six months since there'd been no more Peter! I had no premonitions; like you, I never really feared for his life. I thought he was safe in Palestine. When I discovered he'd been in acute danger for four years I was only grateful that four years' anxiety had been spared me. Because now, I thought, it's all over, and then, a fortnight later, the news reached me. It said Peter had been killed by a grenade. Instantly. His face, it seems, was totally disfigured.[17] He earned certain distinctions, he was one of the veterans of de Gaulle's army and a

[17]According to the chaplain, Peter had been killed by a bursting shell and had not been disfigured. And yet his mother is surely referring to his letter here. I've not been able to trace the contradiction, but it is possible that the chaplain was guilty of a pious lie and that Else had subsequently received other information (this letter to Pitt was written in 1946).

good comrade. I was also informed of his place of burial—a village in Alsace—and that his few belongings are in Paris. Read his letters—the last very long one, the ones from Portugal, the ones from Greece, also the ones he wrote to Ilse Hirsch with whom he formed a very tender friendship (he went to Jerusalem whenever he had leave), and finally the letters from Ilse herself in which she talks about Peter, and you'll be able to learn something about your son, get to know him a little. But it's not much really.

It's months now since I've been waiting for them to send his belongings. Perhaps he left some manuscripts. But I doubt it, how would he have had time? His one desire was to write, so Ilse tells me. So all that our brave, gifted and beautiful child will have left us is a few objects and a few papers wrapped up in a small parcel. Ilse wrote, "I never saw such a handsome man."

Your letter did me good and I love you very much because you're Peter's father. That's why I've told you things in this letter that I've never told anyone else. No one need know. Goodbye.

Your Else

Mind you send back the letters, Pitt.

Garmisch, 2 April 1948[18]

Dear Pitt,

I was summoned to the French Consulate in Munich and was given Peter's belongings.

[18]Peter's mother had returned to Germany a few months previously and was living with Erich Schrobsdorff, who had remarried, and his second wife in Garmisch-Partenkirchen. See below, p. 160.

Everything was tied up in a piece of silk. A bundle of letters from Liena, from Ilse, from his sisters, from me. In a sealed envelope some foreign money, his engagement ring, and a little gold chain from Ellen—"Everybody loves you."[19] Some marching orders, a comb, a fountain pen, a lock of Liena's hair. A small album of photographs of Liena, Sergette, the children, and himself (identity photos). A little case full of badges of all countries, probably taken from men killed in battle—including swastikas and eagles of the Reich. Two pocket watches, two Jewish prayer books, a silver star of David, two other books. His passport and documents.

Write to me, Pitt. You've got to help me. I shan't be able to bear it.

Yours ever,
Else

It's now more than three years.

[19]In English in the text.

I have purposely introduced Peter's letters with only brief introductory notes, designed to explain the sequence of events. I personally knew none of the people who figure in this correspondence and who today are nearly all dead. The information I have gathered about them was provided by Angelika and Ilse (Ilse Yallon since she remarried), but especially by Angelika. The letters to Peter from his mother—the ones written to him in Portugal and Greece—have disappeared. Did he confide them to safekeeping before going to the front? I do not think so, and had he done so he would have entrusted them to Ilse. It is more likely that he had them with him through all his campaigns and that his mother took possession of them again in 1948 when Peter's personal belongings were handed over to her.[20] *Did she then lose them, destroy them? Who knows?*[21] *With the exception of the four letters we have just read, we have so far made the mother's acquaintance only through her son's letters to her. They tell us much and very little. Much because Peter never talks in*

[20]See the letter above to Pitt: "a bundle of letters from Liena, from Ilse, from his sisters, from *me* . . ."

[21]The fact that we have the mother's answer to Peter's long letter is because it never arrived. She had sent this letter to Jerusalem asking Ilse to forward it. But when Ilse received it she already knew that Peter was dead.

monologues, he asks and answers questions, and the questions he asks are searching, pointed, repetitive, urgent, enabling us to form a pretty shrewd guess at the sort of answers and silences they elicited. Moreover Peter was so utterly sincere as he carved out his thoughts and life in solitude, away from all set paths, his self-discipline and good faith were so total, his love so exacting yet unconditional, that his letters are naturally telling, revealing; they allow us to read between the lines, to see that Peter's mother is suppressing some things because it is dangerous to talk, and others for more essential reasons; to see that she sometimes cites an objective danger as an alibi so as to forestall more probing questions. Because of Peter's respect for the freedom of others and because of his relentless endeavour to communicate at a time when everything, both within and without, seems to present an obstacle, we come to distinguish in the course of his letters the sometimes clear, sometimes blurry outlines of a woman's portrait. Rather like Giacometti's haunted figures, who seem to be born far beyond the canvas and remain at a distance that contradicts our perception whether we move towards them or away—so Peter's mother is at once distinct and nebulous, near and far, real and unreal. We know that we could have a clearer picture of her, and yet perhaps not a closer one, and that if we were to know more about her this additional knowledge would not seriously modify the general and contradictory idea we have formed of her. From the first letter we are plunged into the heart of things, into the complex texture of life; and if an area of obscurity remains, it derives as much from the enigma of life as a whole as from lack of information. In other words, communication is indivisible; the son has only to talk to his mother for her to talk to us, and if we use our romantic imagination to fill in the areas of ignorance, we can penetrate almost effortlessly into her universe and make her tragic progress our own. In this sense Peter's letters are self-sufficient and it was unnecessary to overload them with biographical material. In any case it would have been absurd to have such material precede the letters, for at that stage it could only have illuminated the unknown by means of the unknown; before getting to know Peter's mother and father and stepfather, before deciding what part they played, before sorting out their relationship with each other, it was essential to know Peter himself. In other words it was essential to have read his letters.

Even so his letters leave many questions unsolved; they take too much for granted; we need more direct information. And though Peter may show a very deep understanding of his mother, he does not let us know her as subject, he does not let us hear her voice. But fortunately there remains a way of discovering more about her; though Else's letters to her son have disappeared, there are others dating from the same period but written to her friends and relatives in Jerusalem—Ilse Hirsch, Paula and Bruno Kirschner. In these she perhaps reveals herself more than she does to Peter—this adolescent who was at once too familiar and too unfamiliar, to whom she no longer really knew how to talk (or had not yet discovered). Hampered by her role as mother, not fully accepting Peter as a valid interlocutor, in any case denying him the right to challenge her, she probably tried to confine herself in her letters to the narrow and reassuring ground of personal news, and so she probably seemed trivial.

In her letters to her friends, on the other hand, she talks on an equal level; she discusses, argues, lays bare her soul, discloses a personality only faintly reflected in the four letters we have just read, written as they were years later and under massive emotional stress.

In the letters that follow she shows herself as highly perceptive, and yet at times dishonest, desperate, violent, hounded by history, knowing she's not facing things squarely yet persisting in not doing so, defending to the last ditch the former goals of her life. Because these letters discuss the same events and questions as Peter's, her voice provides a priceless counterpoint to his. Also the perspective is reversed, the point of view is changed—here we see the mother judging Peter, and though the truth about Peter we have already accepted remains intact, it is given a different emphasis, enriched with new facets, rooted at a different level. Her failure to appreciate her son's decision, and her hostility towards it, confer on his commitment a dimension we had not yet fully perceived. Peter's vision and his leap towards freedom, Else's blindness and her disruptive rear-guard action (which have their own equally deep reasons) act as a foil to each other, and appear to be complementary parts of one and the same destiny, that of a family crossed by history and marked by tragedy in each of its members. Indeed we could perhaps push the comparison further and discuss Peter's story in the light of the subsequent one of his sisters, Angelika and Bettina. But this is not my province, and, rather than tackle the impossible task of biography (impossible because only distance and a novelistic re-creation would enable me to place these unplaceable, these displaced persons, and really do justice to the constant interaction between the most rigorous subjectivity and the restraints of history), I shall let these new letters—as I let the others—speak for themselves, and just consign to footnotes the explanations that seem indispensable, and were given me by Angelika.

But some of the mother's letters reveal that she underwent a metamorphosis in the course of the years.

Her correspondents in this context are Pitt and Enie, Pitt's second wife. Growing old, at the mercy of an incurable disease, battered by Peter's death and other ordeals and yet delivered from her role as mother, Else in these letters looks on her life and the world with a pitiless eye, and reaches a sombre greatness that seems to equal her son's.

I am also publishing two letters from Erich Schrobsdorff (Angelika's father and Peter's stepfather) which also speak for themselves. And finally some letters from Peter to Ilse written during the war; they complement his mother's and seem to me of capital importance.

From Elisabeth Lingorska[22] *to Ilse Hirsch*
Sofia, July 1939

[. . .] Nothing could have prepared us for what happened at the beginning of November;[23] it absolutely broke me. Up till then I was full of fight, obsessively I repeated to myself, I'll come out of it, I won't give up, I'll pull through. And even if it was sometimes a true hell, even if you can't understand, Ilse, and speak of cowardice, even if I too — first sometimes, then more often and finally nearly all the time — wanted with all my strength to leave, to be free, because I couldn't go on being treated like a dog, now that I've left I know one thing: That in spite of everything my life in Ger-

[22]Through her Bulgarian marriage Peter's mother had become a Lingorska, and had changed her first name from Else to Elisabeth.
[23]"Crystal Night", 9 – 10 November 1938, and the decrees promulgated as a result.

many was my real life, that I ought to have stayed and I would have come through. These last months have proved me right and I regret what I've done, I regret it. Not that I'm homesick exactly, but I shouldn't have given in for my children's sake for I've thrown them into confusion, disarray, disorder, doubt, and myself with them. Erich and I didn't know what to do. The new decrees seemed intolerable and so we came to this conclusion, a painful one for both of us—that we should divorce. And so I re-married and for three months have been here (in Bulgaria). Now I learn that the November decrees wouldn't have affected us, neither me nor the children. Under the influence of anguish and despair I took a decision that I bitterly regret. Only now do I realise what I've lost in Erich. Though I haven't really lost him, indeed from a certain point of view I've got him back by my act, which was 75 percent for his sake.[24] But the bitter feeling remains that I let my hand be forced and that I gave in against my will. Things always go wrong for me when I listen to others instead

[24]The fact is that Erich Schrobsdorff's parents and brothers, who even before the advent of Nazism had formally disapproved of his marriage with a Jewish woman, had been putting increasing pressure on him to divorce since Hitler's rise to power. The Schrobsdorffs, a rich and influential Prussian family, who built and owned hundreds of blocks of flats across Germany, constituted a close-knit clan linked to the new regime by a number of specific economic and political interests. Erich's mother had even thought it necessary to join the Nazi party.

Her son finally yielded to the law and the interests of the clan. It must be said in his defence that he and Else had been living very freely for several years. And also that the pet name *Der Gute* ["the good one" or "the Old Man"] which she had given him was not undeserved; throughout the period of their emigration he helped and protected Else, Angelika, and Bettina to the utmost of his ability. He abandoned them only at the very end, when communication became impossible. After that Else and the girls lived in great poverty.

of following my own instinct. And what now? I don't know. Everything will be settled in the autumn. Perhaps I shall go back—I can, now that I'm Bulgarian. Or perhaps I'll stay and have the children with me here. Nothing has been decided. And my parents are alone, they can't get out, they're 76 . . .

[*From the same letter*]

[. . .] Why do you refuse to understand that people exist who do not share your enthusiasm for Palestine?[25] If it were a haven of peace and quiet, perhaps, but that's not the case as I know it. And as for "safety" . . . For example I think Peter is an imbecile. He left because he thought it was necessary. But he could have stayed, his sisters did, didn't they? But his lordship was too old for that, he didn't want to stay, it was his way of seeing things, his right, he was proud of it. Fair enough. But what about his conversion? Why? To what end? Can he become a Jew? He isn't religious. Nor is he a Zionist. He would never dream of going to Palestine. The result—he's ruining his opportunities for no rhyme or reason. He could have made himself useful, he could have helped us, but he's doing just the opposite. He's behaving like a madman. All that is just dishonest blahblah. His revolt and all the rest which have always been 75 percent for his own comfort. Peter knows my views on the matter. We love each other but I'll never stop telling him he's stupid. Proclamations, narcissism. That's enough of Peter [. . .]

[25]Ilse, a convinced Zionist, had emigrated to Palestine in 1936, taking her husband and two sons with her, and also her father, Professor Mayer, a well-known Berlin pediatrician and the Schrobsdorff children's doctor, who had himself been loath to go. At the time there had been bitter arguments between Else and Ilse, who was thirteen years younger than Peter's mother.

[From the same letter]

[. . .] As for me, I'm doing nothing as usual. I've been spoiled for too long. Difficult and unpleasant tasks have always been spared me and now I'm probably incapable of knuckling down to a life of work, much as I would like to. At first I had to take myself in hand, get my bearings, try to see things clear, that was the most urgent thing. But now my dear ones, the people I love best in the world (Erich, Angelika, Bettina), are due to arrive, which will be another excuse for not working. The truth is that I'm lazy and frivolous, my talents and capacities have never been used as they could have been. And there's no one to help me put this right. I've lots of friends here, I'm very much in demand and from time to time loved. It serves no purpose being as old as I am,[26] everyone calls me Mademoiselle, they take a fancy to me, they fall in love with me, they find me amusing, witty. What an illusion!

From Elisabeth Lingorska to Paula Kirschner[27]
Sofia, March 1940

[. . .] Right, I shall try yet again to get him [Peter] out,[28] but it won't be any good. He drives me to despair, as always, he doesn't change, he doesn't get any wiser. He wants the impossible against all odds, he's a victim of big words. He and I are just like each other in

[26]Else was forty-four at this time.
[27]Paula Kirschner, wife of Dr Bruno Kirschner (see the following letter), was Else's first cousin. The Kirschners had settled in Jerusalem in 1935. Paula is still living there—she is now eighty-six.
[28]Of his Portuguese prison.

this respect; we lie to ourselves with pretty phrases, we escape from reality with pretty phrases. All that is over for me now and doesn't help me any more; I've paid too dear. Although I have to admit, now that I've become honest and clear-sighted (more so than Peter, but I'm a little older, aren't I) that people have shown me a great deal of kindness . . .

From Elisabeth Lingorska to Bruno Kirschner
Sofia, 1 April 1940

Dear Bruno,

Peter's been in Lisbon a year and a half, he's declared himself a Jew, he's been expelled, he spent four months in prison because he hadn't the means to leave the country, he was sent by the Portuguese Committee (Commisar Portuguesa de Anistamiatos Judeus Refugiados) to Greece—the only way of getting him free after all other attempts failed. I paid for it all by giving up the financial support of a friend of mine in Rio. And now I receive a letter from Peter in which he reveals for the first time his true situation. Up to now he maintained an obstinate reticence, always proclaiming optimism. But this letter is desperate. Nothing in view, no money, no residence permit, no work permit. Nothing new, nothing extraordinary, but he's my son! I don't know what to decide; you know me, Bruno, maybe you can help him out? He asks for nothing but to be left in peace and to work. I'm in a ghastly state of anxiety, I keep repeating to myself that I have to do something for him. I must, but I can't. To have him come here is impossible; he would drag us down and the three of us would be brought down with him.[29] The Committee has shown much interest in Peter, even though he's only a "half"; they admire him for the brave line he has

[29]It's clear that Else was terrified by the idea of her son coming to join her in Bulgaria. And that she also did everything she could to delay her own trip to Greece, so that in the end she wouldn't have to go (it is also obvious that she herself invented the story of the five thousand leva—and Peter must have been aware of it—and in any case she admitted in her letter to Ilse of 17 July 1945 that she "would perhaps have gone if [she] had been more energetic"), but her motivations elude us. We know that she was frightened. But of what exactly? We detect that she was frightened in general, frightened of everything, because events overwhelmed her, because she was incapable of living and making decisions alone, because she did not really consent to the break with Germany, because she allowed to be imposed on her an extraordinary exile in a country allied to the Axis; but we do not know what practical consequences this situation entailed for her. The truth is that her generalised fear probably fixed itself onto a very concrete fear: namely that Peter, who was spreading publicly his conversion to Judaism, would not take easily to the secret by which she and her daughters were living in Bulgaria; not having been told they were half-Jewish, the two girls passed for Germans in the eyes of the Bulgarians, at the same time they had been ordered to avoid all contact with citizens of the Reich, who abounded in Bulgaria at that time. They did not understand the reason for this prohibition—the mother imposed silence by cries and tears. A little later, when the Wehrmacht entered Sofia, she lived in constant fear that, for instance, a soldier might ask Angelika directions to somewhere and that the girl—homesick for her father and her country—would answer eagerly in very pure German, and that this would lead to developments beyond her control. So Peter represented an objective danger in Sofia. But he also represented a subjective danger for his mother, for he threatened her in her innermost reality and, as I see it, this is why she never went to Athens; she knew that there would be arguments and that her son would force her to look her situation in the face, to consecrate in her heart her break both with Berlin and with Erich Schrobsdorff—and she was not yet ready for this.

taken and they've backed him up as if he were one of their family—that's what they told me in one of their letters. Perhaps there's still some hope from that quarter. I'm writing in a rather muddled way, but I've reached the end. I've been torturing myself with this business for weeks. It's difficult for you too, I know, and I don't know your situation, but I've got to try everything, everything. I often think about you, and about Paula, and I implore her to help me.

Yours ever,
Else

Happily Father has been spared all this.

Some letters from Peter's mother to Pitt and Enie, all written after Peter's death.

From Else to Pitt
Sofia, 17 August 1946

[. . .] At the last minute and though I am already utterly broken, Erich has administered the coup de grâce and so finished what the Nazis began. He now has the blonde Aryan he was always dreaming of. Taking advantage of the fact that I couldn't do anything about it even by letter, he lost no time in marrying the energetic L., or he let himself be married to her, which amounts to the same thing.[30] So you see, the "Figaro

[30]She had just heard in a letter from Erich Schrobsdorff that he had remarried at the end of the war and that his new wife was one of their common friends.

Lady"[31] has won—all right, I'm unfair, she's got more to her than that and after all there are excuses. But nevertheless he has poisoned the moment we have all been waiting for so long, the moment about which you wrote, "and the day you come back will be a day of rejoicing for all of us!" That he should rob me of this day, after the others had already robbed me of everything else, no, I cannot forgive him for that. So I shall be alone and, frankly, it's all the same to me.

Erich understands nothing about all the things that have happened. He seems to have changed very much and more's the pity. Perhaps he doesn't even realise what he has done to me, but I find it hard to believe. He pretends to make light of everything because he has a guilty conscience, and that's the truth of it [. . .]

[*From the same letter*]

[. . .] It's just possible that my mother died a natural death,[31] but if so she must have tortured herself to death mentally. And I've been a bad daughter just as I've been a bad wife and a bad mother. I've never taken my duties seriously—have I even known what it meant to do so? Duty was an unpleasant burden, so it had to be rejected. Have I ever really achieved anything at all? Hasn't everything been silliness, frivolity, levity, thirst for pleasure, erotic delight, selfishness? Do you see your faults as clearly as I see mine, and do they torture you? Mine torture me. Wherever I look I see only my shortcomings, and nothing I've been able to do seems to have been worth while. And yet now and again I feel I don't even regret it. Because it *was* lovely, wasn't it?

[31] In German "Figaro Dame"—an expression denoting someone as a person with petit-bourgeois ideals.
[32] She died at Theresienstadt in 1943.

From Else to Pitt
Sofia, 8 December 1946

[. . .] I foresaw it all. I foresaw what you would feel and your reactions to Peter's photograph and letters. I was of two minds as to whether to send them to you. Your sorrow for our Peterlein made me so happy and I knew the letters, far from deepening your sorrow or strengthening your love, would somehow disappoint you. Yet you had to know what Peterlein's life was like. As for that remark concerning you, my God, Peter was still so young, young less in years, perhaps, than in his enthusiasms and radicalism.[33] I think this remark expressed a resentment (conscious or unconscious) that he harboured against you, a purely personal resentment that started in his childhood when, unfortunately, you weren't a friend to him. He wasn't mature enough to understand you and to realise what had made you like that. You yourself often reproach yourself with this so you can hardly be cross with me for bringing it up again. We were so mad! And even I can't cry in peace and quiet knowing I always did the right thing by my Peterlein. And this is what makes everything so unbearable. We were far too thoughtless! Yes, and because he felt such a wholehearted hatred for the Germans, and because he also wanted to be a little unfair to you out of revenge—such a trivial and puerile revenge—he mixed up everything together and wrote that sentence. There, that's what I think, but of course I may be wrong [. . .]

[33]See Peter's letter of 31 May 1939: "It is sad, infinitely sad, that a man like my father should spend his life writing plays for the people."

[*From the same letter*]

[. . .] I went on feeling that Germany was my fatherland for several years more—the Germany where mind and spirit flourished. I said to myself, "It's my country, my language, the land where my roots are, the land where I belong." But I suppose I'm really a Jew after all; I don't need Germany any more.[34] What Germany gave me I've still got; I love the German language, music, books, the various people to whom I was devoted and whom I understand as I shall never understand anyone in any other country. But all that is over now. I'm somewhere else altogether. I shall be a stranger among you,[35] and what I would have been ready to die for before means nothing to me now, it will leave me cold. Everything has become so dreadfully unimportant to me, so petty; I see and feel right through things and people, it's a very uncomfortable state to be in! But perhaps I'm wrong, perhaps the past will come to life again; perhaps it's only a passing reaction to what I've suffered, a "moment of weakness" as my father put it. I feel I can live anywhere at all,

[34]The daughter of successful tradespeople, liberal yet deeply attached to the traditions of Judaism, Else was already engaged to a rich Jewish businessman when she met the poet Schwiefert, whose indifference to practical matters, vast knowledge, and lyrical plays fascinated her. She jilted the businessman and went off with Fritz Schwiefert and married him. The Kirschner parents, outraged both by her callousness and by her marriage to a penniless *goy* poet, denied her access to their home and money. They relented only with the birth of Peter, an event which put the seal on their reconciliation. In fact Else acted no differently from many German Jewish women; she threw herself with passion into the adventure of assimilation at the very moment when anti-Semitism, always deep-rooted, was about to break out with redoubled force.

[35]At the time of this letter Else was preparing to return to Germany.

provided it's beautiful and that I've got my children and a little money. And even here in Bulgaria, if you can imagine. What do theatres matter? I never step inside one anymore. To be with you, whom I love, that's enough, it's all I ask for. But I'm ashamed because I shall just sit in a chair and say nothing. My face is now half-paralyzed and it's very difficult for me to talk. It's a cruel blow. So many thoughts come into my mind and I have to keep silent!

From Else to Pitt
Garmisch, 13 January 1948[36]

[. . .] I once asked you in one of my letters if there was a God, and you denied it then. And now that you seem to have found him, I have lost him. It was that deep belief inside me that sustained me during all the years of my emigration. How else do you imagine I could have borne it? I often made calculations, it's true. How about you? We all do. And it's also true that I made things easy for myself by not "asking" sincerely, I only really asked for absurd things. In fact I've never been very good at calculating and more than once I've lost my way in my accounts. The balance at any rate is bad. You write, don't ask for more than people can give you. Whether I ask or not the result is exactly the same, and it's not I who am wrong to ask too much, it's the others. They're incapable of giving because their hearts are mean and they've forgotten everything. I've the

[36]Else had now been back in Germany for a few months and was living at Garmisch-Partenkirchen with Erich Schrobsdorff and his second wife, L. Pitt lived in Berlin.

right to ask because I've suffered more than all of you and if no one is able or willing to help me, very well, I'll put up with that too, as I've put up with everything else. It isn't important.

My face wasn't bathed in tears on Peter's birthday, nor was it on the 7th. The 5th and the 7th are no worse than the 16th. Anyway, I seldom cry. Even if I can't get over my remorse, at least I can try not to indulge in self-pity because that's a miserable thing. However I do pity myself sometimes and I sometimes cry [. . .]

From Else to Pitt
Garmisch, 26 May 1948

[. . .] Yes, I've consulted another doctor and it's what I feared. Don't worry, of course nothing can be done. The Berlin doctor whom we thought a fool has turned out to be right.[37] I knew it in my heart of hearts but I wanted to hide the truth from myself. It's an absolutely unexplored incurable disease[38] and my only hope is that it won't spread, that it will remain static, though I don't believe much in that either. The professor assures me this is possible, though very exceptional, and why on earth should I be an exception? It's true that I've often been an exceptional case—and this disease is a proof of it—but it's easier, isn't it, to be exceptional in bad things than in good? Besides I feel this rare and strange affliction to be in some way just. I've always had an insight into my illnesses and I recognise their meaning. So it only remains for me to

[37]She had been to Berlin to consult a specialist.
[38]Multiple sclerosis.

resign myself to the inevitable and this is not what's most difficult. The most difficult thing is fear. My mother used to say, "It's not so terrible to have to leave the world, what's tough is *how* to leave it." But that's enough of that. After all it was marvellous while it lasted. And others have suffered more. As for the few years that have still got to take their toll, don't worry, I shall get through them [. . .]

From Else to Enie Schwiefert
Gauting, 3 August 1948[39]

[. . .] I'm now living on a different plane from you,[40] in another universe. These last ten years—or is it twelve by now?—have been so fundamentally different for me, have so changed me, that objectivity has deserted me; all my hatred goes against the Germans, and as far as I'm concerned the victors can do what they like, I'll always make excuses and allowances for them even if I believed all the reproaches poured down on them. I used to live in the deepest friendship with the BBC and when it was torture to get up in the morning I consoled myself with the thought that in the evening I'd be able to listen in to the radio and England. And I viewed Churchill as a great genius and wholeheartedly admired the way they conducted their war and the humanity with which they treated the Jews—no, I neither could nor would want to forget it.

[39]Gauting, a place near Munich.

[40]The two women had known each other in Berlin when Else was still married to Fritz Schwiefert.

And I'm not against the Russians either. Perhaps it's my Bulgarian past, but I feel very much at home in one big room and I like simple people much better than so-called gentlemen. I also think that all the old ideas and attitudes are worn out and utterly devoid of meaning; people who aren't capable of renouncing them seem to me non-people, they strike false and hollow. Here I'm looked on as a "Red" and I often have violent arguments with Erich. At least I did at first, but not any more. I find the Germans intolerable, the way they give vent to cheerful indignation at every Russian act of violence — as if it justified their own crimes — and of course it's still the fault of the Jews, they're ready to bring that back with their "hurrahs"; and other countries have never experienced anything but fear and envy before them, these matchless Germans . . . I tell you this: If the occupation came to an end, it would only take a year for us to fall back into the former filth! [. . .]

[*From the same letter*]

[. . .] We haven't any money either and yet we've bought the house because that's how L. wanted it. Erich has a lot of worries, all the talk here is of restrictions and economies, sometimes it's hardly bearable. What's the good of buying a house if you have to deprive yourself of everything so as to live in it? But what matters is that we're now housed "in style". And why? If you really want to know, it's just "for show". And Gauting is such a foul place. In any case, Enie, *you* can be happy. Remember that you haven't lost anything and your health is good. Even at sixty, one can enjoy life. It occurs to me that there's no hardship in growing old provided one keeps one's wits and one's health. I've never known what it was to be really ill,

I'm only discovering now. And what an illness! I'm in shreds, I've got terribly thin, my hands aren't at all as they should be, and my general weakness and the state of my heart are a real torture. I walk very very slowly, the best is not to walk at all, and I don't know where it's going to lead me. But enough of that, it's boring [. . .]

From Else to Pitt and Enie
Gauting, 18 February 1949

I'm very ill and I don't think I've got much longer. My whole body is affected now and my heart is giving up too. I'm so thin that by comparison I was fat and in good form last time you saw me! I'm utterly weak and can't really do anything any more. I've not been equal to it.

Yours ever,
Else

From Erich Schrobsdorff to Fritz Schwiefert[41]
Kiel, 17 March 1946

[. . .] Peter's the only one of us not to survive. Peter died in action right at the end, as a soldier in de Gaulle's army. Where, on what exact date, and in what circumstances the note doesn't say.

[41]Having been informed of Peter's death in a laconic note from Else, Erich Schrobsdorff tracked down Fritz Schwiefert and sent him the following letter. The two men had known each other for a long time;

My dear Pitt, I've never been so shattered by a letter before, never been left so devoid of thoughts and words. Perhaps it's because in a case like this only the heart can speak. It's such an utterly unexpected blow, such an unforeseeable stroke of fate, a blow that none of us could possibly have imagined, and so out of harmony with his whole life and being. Peter a soldier, Peter bearing arms, Peter in combat, combat crowned with a warrior's death! It presents the boy in such a strange light that the mind boggles and it's all I can do to believe it. And yet he must have followed this path with his eyes wide open, otherwise he wouldn't have volunteered to join de Gaulle's army.

Oh, sorrow cries out so much louder than words! Into what fathomless depths must Else have sunk when she received the appalling news! Her total love for her only son, the son she loved more and more each year and whom she so longed to have with her, all her hopes of finally finding a haven of peace for the evening of her life, in a happier country, and with him, with a mature and purified Peter who had become the centre of all her thoughts . . . nothing can have any meaning or purpose for her any more. This most cruel of all her ordeals has fallen on her just when she thought her sufferings were drawing to an end. I'm terribly sad not to be able to be with her at a time like this.

And neither can I come to see you, to clasp your hand. Because we wouldn't need to speak, would we? We'd just meditate a while and think about the past when he was still with us. Although he was often very difficult and often gave us cause for anxiety, he was at bottom a young man of perfect loyalty, full of heart

---

Erich had met Else at one of the many parties that took place in the Schwieferts' home in Berlin in the chaotic days after the First World War.

despite his selfishness, infinitely gifted and with immense intellectual vitality. You too, like Else, must have been thinking about a new age, when everything would be different, a time in the near future when life would bring together what it had so brutally and absurdly torn apart—even if at first it was only a reunion in spirit, an exchange of ideas or a brief personal encounter. This is how I think about Angelika and all my hopes reach out towards that goal. What ineffable sadness if this sustaining hope were to collapse and end in nothingness.[42] And it's in the same spirit that I think of you, as a friend and as a father, because in spite of all our disagreements I was close to that boy and I tried to form and serve his destiny—even if I was clumsy and often made mistakes, I honestly tried.

But everything has turned out differently. This period of tragedy and upheaval that has more or less torn our lives to pieces, coincided with his youth. We were far too occupied with ourselves to deal properly with his upbringing; and we were either too old or too young to be companions that he couldn't challenge. And so it was that under pressure of inner conflicts that threatened to tear him apart he ended up going his own way. He hoped by his flight to escape the tensions he carried about within him, but life led him implacably to take his place in the front line among soldiers fighting for our existence, to preserve for it some meaning and goal. There was no escape route, this led him right through to the final, the most real consequence. By falling on the battlefield side by side with those he felt to be his own in spirit and blood, he gave the deepest justification and ultimate significance to the choice he had made for his life after so much questing, erring and dreaming. He became a fighter for freedom.

[42]Angelika returned to Germany a year later, in 1947.

From Erich Schrobsdorff to Fritz Schwiefert
Gauting, 9 October 1949

[. . .] I had always hoped that poor Schnuff would be comforted by the life and animation we created around her, that it would be some sort of compensation for all that had been taken from her. But, alas, her illness was too strong; her love for our little Viola[43] served no purpose really, our little will-o'-the-wisp became too tiring for her towards the end. She became indifferent to our pretty house and lovely garden in the final months, and even the sun, which she had always adored, was too strong, too intense, it exhausted her. Of course we did everything to help Schnuff forget her tragedy. It wasn't easy, for there was a lot of bitterness in her and she refused the hand we held out to her. Her last attempt to find faith—by joining the Orthodox Church—unfortunately turned out to be a failure. Her intellect was stronger. She then put all her hope in an Allied victory which she tried to look on as the victory of reason. But here again she was disappointed, because the division of the world into two blocs, East and West, took away her last comfort and support. She started to waver between East and West, between faith and reason, between us and Bulgaria (she often wondered whether she'd been right to leave Bettina)[44] and, coming back after so long, she laid herself open to inevitable disappointment; she started getting more and more like her mother who also barricaded herself behind refusal towards the end of her life and saw

[43]A daughter he had had three years previously by his second wife, L.

[44]Bettina, who had married and was the mother of two children, was the only one to stay in Bulgaria.

nothing but the meaninglessness of the world. After the terrible battering she had had, it is understandable that she consciously chose to cut herself off from everything. I don't think there's any effective treatment for her disease now available, and yet I never stop reproaching myself and telling myself that we didn't do enough for her, and that with more sacrifices we might perhaps have won.

You are right when you point out how inconceivable it seems that this creature, who was life itself, should be reduced to nothingness. When I visit her grave I often have a feeling of unreality, as if a part of myself were buried there. It is impossible to forget her, for it was around her that our circle was formed and held together; she was its head and its heart.

And finally, some letters from Peter to Ilse Hirsch written in the course of the war (in Peter's original English).

15 November 1941

. . . And though our opinions differ somewhat in that matter [Israel] I am talking with great emphasis of Palestine. You see, Ils'chen, we had a conversation about that, but I couldn't say what I really meant. I don't know why. Maybe it's because I've been alone for years and saying things, such as they are, is difficult for me. But one thing is very clear to me: political and human ideals must be cosmopolitan. There is no use of sticking together in families, communities, nations. The fact in itself is natural, but it must be considered as a basis and not as an end. If you take it as the first, the way is free for evolution and development, but in the second case, people are limiting themselves voluntarily, are getting narrow-minded and finish up with patriotism. And it needs a nation of strongest discipline, self-control and a centuries-old experience to keep such a spirit in bounds. That the fewest can, you see in what Europe has become. But if there is a human group that —by its history is cosmopolitan in face and in spirit— no matter whether by force or of own will, that has overcome a certain stage of human existence and has developed into a higher one—a group that is an example, a terrible one by the process they had to endure in order to become what they are and by the still lasting sufferings, yet a wonderful one by the demonstration of what mankind is capable of—if such people exist, why apply on them old proceedings and old forms which cannot lead them but into a backwards movement. Why are you trying to build up a nation when it's not at all desirable to do so. Nations! We have enough of them! Why to create a people of human material that has no other mission than getting their "patria" flag and national anthem? You may say, it's necessary. Yes, it is necessary to give people help and lead them somewhere and in that way Palestine has my whole approval as much as any other country being of good will. I can hear your objection: "Palestine first and above all, for it's 'Eretz Israel'. Jews can't be safe and happy but there. Do you know something about American anti-Semitism?"

I am answering: "You certainly know something anti-Semitism in Palestine and about the difficulties Jews encounter in that country!"

The task would thus be the same: elimination of anti-Semitism and education of mankind regarding tolerance and esteem for each other. That's quite a general task, I guess. In Palestine not less problematic than in America. And seen from this point of view, rescuing the victims of intolerance can be done without the application of all this national stuff, as it is done all over the world. Why must the Jews have a "national home"? They mustn't. They must live among other people to stay fully conscious of their identity. There must be someone to do this job, it's a very important one . . .

16 September 1942

[. . .] I'm in a very bad mood, Ils'chen, and utterly unsatisfied with myself and my doings. That is, unsatisfied with doing exactly nothing and that's the trouble. I'm afraid, I'll never start writing if things go on like this. I've got plans and ideas and an ardent desire to get them down on paper. Every day my first and last thought is: "You must write, you've got to, why don't you do it . . . "And then—nothing. Suddenly no words, no coherent thought any more, everything is becoming more and more vague and progressively annihilating itself. The slightest disturbance (and in that sort of life I'm living, there aren't but disturbances), makes me give up before I begin. I realise I can't, I'm incapable of doing anything. Everything is an obstacle, the very desire to write is an obstacle. It's absurd. I'm completely lacking any sort of calm and concentration and initiative. I'm dreaming, that's all. And doing nothing. And always, every hour, every minute nearly, the same shameful feeling of neglected duty and the ridiculousness of saying "I can't". But if I want it so much and more than anything in the world, why can't I? What is it exactly, that hinders me? Is it only the outside world, my being a soldier, having no place to be alone and a thousand disturbances a day? Or is it in me, in my very mind; or is it utter laziness, a supreme phlegma; or is it that things are not ripe yet, that the only means is still to wait, patiently, or oh, I don't know . . . It's more than ridiculous, sometimes I'm feeling like being crippled. And at other times there is a great fear; if really I don't succeed in doing it, in getting into work somehow, if definitely I'm unable to write—what have I got left to do? I'm purposeless then, perfectly useless . . .

30 November 1942

[. . .] In one point you are wrong, Ils'chen: the fact of having had too good a life in my youth has nothing to do with my particular problem (of not being able to write) and as to the general conditions of life and their effect on me, I can perfectly take the war as much as I could take three years of refugee existence—most perfectly. Since the day of my emigration and the profound change within me, my morals have at no moment and not in the slightest been affected by any hardships whatsoever. I even pretend that my spirits have ever since been much higher than that of a lot of other people living under the same conditions and will continue to be higher. There have never been any regrets concerning the road I took. I have just obeyed my own decisions and determinations, for from the beginning on, I've been completely conscious of its implications and consequences . . .

29 January 1943

[. . .] Here we are—at last! Victory is a good thing—especially, when you are not particularly in the habit of it—Montgomery is a dear and life not so bad after all—the simple physical life, I mean, with fresh meals to eat, wine to drink, water to wash, trees and green about and the well-doing atmosphere in somehow inhabited areas. Not bad at all for an old desert-dog who used to look upon the world as primarily made of sand and found it quite natural to have the precious material continually and carefully distributed all over his body, in mouth, nose, ears, eyes, stomach, mind, and other places as well. Thus I am saluting with adequate satisfaction and enthusiasm a new epoch of life and war. Keeping only a faint reminiscence of the by-gone (let's hope so!) pleasures and delights the so-called WD[45] bestowed upon us with such generosity . . .

29 September 1943

[. . .] I'm on guard in a tiny Arab village[46] with nothing but Arabs and nothing but flies and unattractive grown-up-looking children and wrapped-in women, whose heavy brown blankets you have not the least desire to lift (for you have learned to guess their faces underneath); and here and there a noise, a quarrel, a cry, the drone of a camel cart between narrow

[45]"WD": abbreviation for "Western Desert"—the desert of Libya. This letter alludes to the entry of the 8th army into Tripoli, after Montgomery's victorious counter-offensive.
[46]In Tunisia.

white-chalked walls, and the sun cutting edgy shadows out of dirty sand, and every now and then a soldier passing by, lazily . . . Oh, I know all this so well—the villages, people, atmosphere, soldiers . . . and my head is empty in the midst of all this voidness. I'm trying to think of something and only get drowsy . . .

25 November 1944

[. . .] Thanks a lot, darling, for your last letter. I know you are never angry with me, but still it makes me feel uneasy to be always so late in writing. Only this time it wasn't my fault; first we were in battle-line in the woods and it rained and rained and rained, and we had little shelter and much sentry duty and patrols and all that stuff; then we were in battle-line again, but somewhere else, 700 metres high, and there was snow. We lived in dug-outs and it was pretty cold and you know, the thing I can stand least is cold. So I was frozen all day long and only pinched a little warmth at night—icy feet and icy hands and shivering, shivering, shivering. Well, and then it was the offensive, attacks, assaults, advance, the whole damned lot, as I said at the beginning, and only now we've come to a standstill and have quite a good time in a little village—a room with a big stove, and straw for a bed, and rabbits and chicken for food, and rest, sleep . . .

8 December 1944

[. . .] I'd very much like to know, what Schnuffo is thinking about it (Bettina's marriage). I'm sure, she didn't develop into a conventional mother and never will. Oh, Ils'chen. I am longing to see her! I want it so much, it sometimes hurts. She's getting old . . . and that's an appalling thought to me. I can't imagine her as an old woman, it isn't her genre. You see, I believe, I'm not a conventional son either — it became clear to me long after I had left her, that she isn't just my mother. I am able to think of her as a woman and I have always cherished this capability and always believed it great. And now she's getting old, that's terribly hard . . .

I'm sure, Ils'chen, you realise what it means to me to know my dear ones are free at last, are on our side now, are no longer unattainable for free and unhampered words — I can speak to them again, I can ask and explain; I can learn the truth, the many realities I am as yet in serious doubt about, and I can say what I feel and am and have become — how deeply I love them, how much I was afraid, how much I longed, how long these years have been and with what unspeakable impatience and anticipation I'm looking ahead to the end of it all, when, if all goes well, I'll be again with them, with her. And we'll look into each other's eyes for a long time (I believe, she will not cry) and we will comprehend, know without explaining, what was the hardest and what it is that truly matters and where we sinned and where we did right and that love has many faces . . . all that, for we are very close to each other, so very much alike . . .

Else, Erich Schrobsdorff, and Fritz Schwiefert died in 1949, 195l and 1953 respectively. All were under sixty years old.

Bettina stayed in Bulgaria until 1969, when homesickness for Germany was too much for her. She is divorced and lives alone and poorly in Munich. Her two children have never left Sofia.

Angelika returned to Germany in 1947 and discovered Israel for the first time in 1960. She began to go there for two months every year. But in 1970 she left Germany—and Europe—for good and now lives in Jerusalem, the only place in the world, she says, where she is not afraid. She is surrounded by Jews from Berlin who are her only family. Ilse is her best friend.

Appendix

In December, 1943, Peter addressed the following "Statement", in English, to the 8th British Army:

Statement
5 December 1943

I, Peter Schwiefert, born on January 5th 1917 in Berlin, Germany of German-Jewish parents (divorced; father still living in Germany, no details known since outbreak of war; mother re-married, Bulgarian nationality, living in Sofia, Bulgaria, present name: Elisabeth Lingorska) of formerly German nationality, the loss of which, by decree of the German Government, was notified to me by the German Legation in Athens, Greece in July 1940—present nationality: none—have emigrated from Germany in September, 1938, living as a refugee in Portugal from this date to March, 1940, and in Athens, Greece until March, 1941. After several attempts to join the British Army (volunteered, since November, 1939, at British authorities in Lisbon, Portugal, later in Greece—entered into the lists for Foreign Volunteers drawn by the British Military Attaché in Athens) which proved altogether unsuccessful. I have then taken to enlist for the Free French Forces (December, 1940, at the French National Committee in Athens), was admitted, with references given by the above mentioned British Military Attaché in Athens, Maj. Hayworth, by Free French Headquarters in Cairo and sent to Egypt, joined up with the Troops Commander by General de Gaulle on March 31st 1941. I have since then served in the Infantry, taking part in all campaigns in which the Free French were engaged (Syrian campaign, 2nd Libyan campaign, Bir-Hakeim, 3rd Libyan-Tunisian campaign). Holding the German Baccalaureate and speaking and writing fluently three languages (English, French, German), I have made several applications to be employed as interpreter, which have all been rejected. Army speciality: driver.

On enlistment, the conditions under which a soldier in the Free French Forces was to serve, were clearly stipulated and stated in a certificate ("Attestation" Français) issued by the British Embassy in Cairo and the French National Committee in Egypt and signed by Mr M.R. Wright on behalf of the Embassy, and Colonel P. S. Dunsmore Captain, on behalf of the British Military Authority, as follows:

" . . . to serve with honour and fidelity in the Forces of General de Gaulle's French National Committee, under British Command . . . (he) is subject to British Military Regulations and recognised as member of the British Military Forces. Until special dispositions settle the question of (his) nationality (he) will be under protection of the British diplomatic and consular authorities to the same degree as a British citizen."

During all the time my unit was thus made part of the British Forces and, as a matter of fact, for long of the Eighth Army, I have had no reason to object to the actual state of affairs. I think I now have: by the union of the French Forces and the formation of a sole French

Peter as a soldier in the Free French Forces.

1

2

3

1. Peter as a child and his mother, in Berlin.
2. Peter, Angelika, Bettina and their mother.
3. Liena.
4. Angelika in Bulgaria.

4

1

1. Fritz Schwiefert, Peter's father.
2. Peter at age five.
3. Erich Schrobsdorff in 1948, three years before his death.
4. Peter in 1937, a year before he leaves Berlin.
5. Peter's mother in 1936.
6. Bettina as a teenager.
7. Peter's mother and Angelika in Varna, Bulgaria (summer of 1939).

2 3

4

5

6 7

1

2

1. Daniel Kirschner, Peter's grandfather on his mother's side.
2. Ilse Hirsch in Berlin.
3. Certificate of the French National Committee of Egypt, admitting Peter as a soldier into the ranks of de Gaulle's army.

No. Matricule 10138

ATTESTATION.
(FRANCAIS).

Le .... (désignation de l'autorité britannique compétente, en principe l'Ambassade) certifie que :

Nom Schwiefert

Prénoms Peter

Né le 5 Janvier 1917

A Berlin (Allemagne)

Fils de Fritz

et de Elisabeth Lingorska (remariée) Kirchener (origine)

Signalement :
Taille : 1.75
Yeux : vert
Front : decouvert
Nez : aquilin
Teint : Clair
Signes particuliers :

s'engage à servir avec honneur et fidélité dans les unités relevant du Comité National Français du Général de Gaulle, sous les ordres du Commandement britannique, à l'exclusion de toute opération contre les forces françaises.

Il est admis dans ces unités avec le grade de soldat de 2° classe à dater du 31 mars 1941 et une ancienneté militaire de néant à la date du présent engagement.

Il est soumis au statut des militaires britanniques, et il est reconnu comme membre des Forces Militaires britanniques.

En attendant que des dispositions particulières règlent la question de la nationalité de l'interessé, celui-ci béneficiera de la protection des autorités britanniques diplomatiques et consulaires au même titre qu'un citoyen britannique.

Date .... 19 ....

Signature de l'Ambassade

M.R. Wright

Signature de l'engagé

Peter Schwiefert

Signature du Representant de l'Autorité Militaire Britannique

C.S. Dinsmore Captain

1

Forces Francaises Libres — Le 22 Juin 1944

Iere D.F.L

EXTRAIT

Par Ordre General N° 83 en date du 22 Juin 1944, le General BROSSET Commandant la Iere Division Francaise Libre Cite:

a l'Ordre de la DIVISION

Soldat de 2eme Classe SCHWIMFERT Peter
Mle IOI38

A participé a toutes les campagnes avec le B.I.M. depuis I940. Employe comme voltigeur dans son groupe, lors de l'attaque du I6 Mai sur le piton a l'ouest de San Giorgio, s'est fait remarqué par son courage et son ardeur pendant tout le combat. A été blessé a l'épaule

La présente Citation Comporte l'attribution de la Croix de Guerre avec Etoile d'Argent

Certifié conforme
Le Capitaine GOLFIER Commandant
la 3eme Cie du B.I.M.P

2

Statement.

I, Peter Schwifert, born on January 5th 1917 in Berlin – Germany of German-Jewish parents (divorced: father still living in Germany, no details known since outbreak of war: mother re-married, Bulgarian nationality, living in Sofia – Bulgaria, present name: Elisabeth Luigorska), of formerly German nationality the loss of which by decree of the German Government was notified to me by the German Légation in Athens – Greece in July 1940 – present nationality: none – have emigrated from Germany in September 1938, living, as a refugee, in Portugal from this date to March 1940, and in Athens – Greece until March 1941. After several attempts to join the British Army (volunteered, since November 1939, at British authorities in Lisbon – Portugal, later in Greece – entered into the lists for Foreign Volunteers drawn by the British Military Attaché in Athens) which proved altogether unsuccessful, I

– 1 –

1. Citation awarding Peter the "Croix de Guerre" with a silver star, from the First Division of the Free French Forces.
2. Peter's "Statement".